Praise for *The Princess Rules*:

'Enchanting, simply written stories that have lost none of their pertinence'

– *Telegraph,* 5 star review ✶✶✶✶✶

'Princess Florizella won't be rescued by a prince, nor will she dress as she is told . . . She breaks the rules, dares to be different and can even see the good in scary giants'

– *The Times,* Best Children's Books of 2019

First published in Great Britain in three separate editions:
Princess Florizella by Viking Kestrel 1988, *Florizella and the Wolves* by Walker
Books Ltd 1991 and *Florizella and the Giant* by Walker Books Ltd 1992
This edition published by HarperCollins *Children's Books* in 2020
HarperCollins *Children's Books* is a division of HarperCollins*Publishers* Ltd,
HarperCollins Publishers
1 London Bridge Street
London SE1 9GF

The HarperCollins website address is
www.harpercollins.co.uk

2

ISBN 978–0–00–833979-1

Philippa Gregory and Chris Chatterton assert the moral right to be identified
as the author and illustrator of the work respectively.
A CIP catalogue record for this title is available from the British Library.

Printed and bound in England by CPI Group (UK) Ltd, Croydon, CR0 4YY

The Princess Rules

PHILIPPA GREGORY

Illustrations by
Chris Chatterton

HarperCollins *Children's Books*

For Freddie and Sebastian

Contents

Princess Florizella

CHAPTER ONE

*Florizella's parents completely
fail to open their windows
for a passing stork to drop
a baby on them*

*O*nce upon a time (that means I don't
exactly know when, but it wasn't that long
ago), in the land called the Seven Kingdoms,
the king and queen very much wanted a son.
They waited and waited until one day the
queen told her husband, 'I have news for you.
We are going to have a beautiful baby boy!'

'And when he grows up he will be king,' said
the king, very pleased. 'What a lovely surprise.'

But when the baby came, it was not a boy. It was a girl.

This was a big shock for the king and queen, but since they were royal they put on a smile and took the baby through the tall windows to the balcony of the palace and waved at everyone. They pretended that they did not mind that she was a girl when they had been counting on a boy, and after a little while they loved her anyway. 'Besides,' the king said, 'undoubtedly she will marry a handsome rich prince, and they can be king and queen over his kingdom and ours. Undootedly!'

'We'll call her Florizella,' said the queen. 'Princess Florizella.'

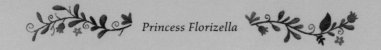

Though they started with good intentions, the king and queen were dreadfully careless parents. They messed up the christening by inviting everyone, so that nobody was furiously offended. No angry witches blew in and put a fatal spell on the baby, nobody turned her into a mouse. The king and queen forgot all about locking her in a high tower so that a prince could climb up her hair to rescue her, they did not forbid her from spinning, or ban her from sharp needles. They did remind her not to run with scissors in her hands, but this is of no use to a fairytale princess – it's just normal. They did not strap her into tight gowns so she had a tiny, tiny waist that a prince could span with one hand. They did not feed her poisoned apples and bury her in a glass coffin. The queen was

particularly neglectful – she completely failed to die and leave her daughter to a cruel stepmother to make her herd geese or sit in the cinders.

They let Florizella do as she liked, and so it was partly their fault that she did not learn the Princess Rules, but grew up into a cheerful, noisy, bossy, happy girl who spent her mornings on her horse called Jellybean, and her afternoons working with them in the royal office. She particularly liked answering letters of complaint about the expense and the unimportance of a royal family. Mostly, she agreed with them. 'We are dretfully ex-pence-sieve' she wrote when she was six years old.

'You're never going to post it like that!' said the king.

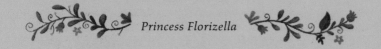
'So sweet,' said the queen, putting it in the bin.

Florizella was friends with some princesses who had studied the Princess Rules, and behaved just as the Rules said they should. Florizella thought their hair was lovely: so golden and so very long! And their clothes were nice: so richly embroidered by devoted peasants. And their shoes were delightful: so tiny and handmade in silk! But their days bored her to death!

In the morning, they got up, washed their faces and put cream on their cheeks and on their hands and on their noses. Then it was time for breakfast. They drank hot water and

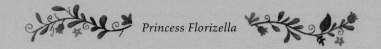

sometimes green tea. The Princess Rules were clear about breakfast: 'Princesses live off air,' the Rules said. They got dressed, and that took them hours because they wore petticoats and underclothes and beautiful gowns and overgowns and even those tall pointy hats called henins. By the time they got all that on, and did their hair, it was lunchtime.

In the afternoon, they were too tired to do anything but pluck their eyebrows.

In the evening, they said they were bored.

'What do *you* do all day?' they asked Florizella, looking in bewilderment at her. She wore trousers and a shirt for riding, and a skirt or a dress for best.

'I'm learning how to run the Seven Kingdoms

when I'm grown up,' she told them. 'I've got a lot of ideas.'

'Ideas!' They were all quite horrified. 'We don't have ideas! We have the Rules.'

But Florizella thought that everyone should live in the size of house that they needed. So families with lots of children, or who had friends living with them, should have the biggest houses, and small families should have the smaller houses.

'Actually, that sounds rather sensible,' said the queen, who was sick of dusting the 134 royal rooms of the palace.

Florizella thought that everyone should be paid whether they had a job or not. They should be paid to garden or think, to paint or run. Fathers could stay at home and look after

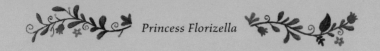

the children, and when mothers went out to interesting jobs they could come home to a clean, tidy house.

'That would never work,' said the king, who had no intention of dusting 134 rooms, not even one or two.

Florizella laughed and went out to canoe in the moat. 'You know, she's not like a regular princess at all,' the king complained to the queen. 'I think you must have gone very badly wrong somewhere.'

'She'll find her own way, in her own time,' the queen said comfortably. 'And surely, since she's a princess born and bred, she'll just naturally come to the Princess Rules in time? Won't she?'

CHAPTER TWO

*Florizella will go to
the ball - no pumpkin
required*

One day an invitation came to the palace. It said *Princess Florizella* on the front in wonderful curly writing. It was an invitation for a ball, to be given by Prince Bennett in the next-door kingdom – the Land of Deep Lakes. He wanted to meet all the princesses in the neighbouring realms so that he could choose one to marry.

'I'd like to go,' said Princess Florizella at

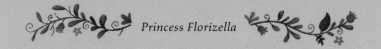

breakfast when the invitation arrived.

The king gave the queen a look, which meant that she must start the job of telling Florizella 'no'.

'I don't think you'd enjoy it,' the queen said nicely.

Florizella said she thought she would.

The queen gave the king *That Look*, and he said, rather impatiently, for he was uncomfortable when he thought he might hurt Florizella's feelings:

'Thing is, Florizella, Prince Bennett will never choose you to be his bride because there will be very, very pretty princesses there, trained in the Princess Rules. And you have never been like that. Not at all.'

'I know that,' said Florizella. 'But I'm not

going there to get married to Prince Bennett. I'm going to see my friends and enjoy the party.'

'Ah,' the king said. 'Then you may go. Undoubtedly. *Undootedly!*'

So she threw a clean pair of jeans in a bag, and after lunch she hopped into the glass coach – for they had no cars and trains or buses in the Seven Kingdoms – and drove off with her horse, Jellybean, trotting behind.

Prince Bennett's kingdom wasn't far from Florizella's home, and Florizella was the first to arrive. The prince had invited one hundred and twenty-one princesses, and Florizella waited at the gate to watch them all drive

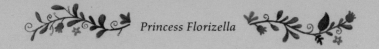

past. One hundred and twenty princesses went by, some in fine carriages, some in smaller ones, and one or two in carts. One very poor princess came in a wheelbarrow. Some of them were very beautiful and some were less so, but they all desperately wanted to marry Prince Bennett. They didn't have anything else to do in those days, and the Princess Rule no. 500 (the last) said: Marry a handsome prince.

The one hundred and twenty-first princess, Florizella, was the only one not planning marriage. She was just there for the party.

'And to eat the food!' said Princess Florizella longingly when she saw the banquet.

She had a wonderful time. There were tons of cakes, and three hundred different sorts of

ice cream and forty different coloured jellies. There were meringues, pizzas and hot dogs. There were sticks of rock and candyfloss. There were toffee apples, and strawberries still growing in the strawberry beds that you could pick yourself and eat – as many as you wanted. Florizella ate a very good dinner indeed.

But the one hundred and twenty princesses ate a little bread and butter and nothing more. They were worried about spilling on their best ballgowns. They were worried about whether they would

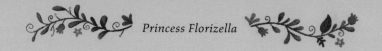

be able to dance lightly on their toes. They were worried that someone might think they were greedy. (Princess Rule no. 42: Princesses Live Off Air.) Florizella worried about nothing. She had seconds and thirds of nearly everything.

She had a much better dinner than Prince Bennett, who had to dance with every single one of the hundred and twenty-one princesses. He thought he had better make an early start. He danced with each princess, one after another, and they all smiled and agreed with whatever he said.

They were lovely. They were the nicest girls he had ever met. They were so pleasant that he could not tell them apart. They were so charming that he had the horrid feeling

that nobody could be that nice *all* the time. So how could he possibly know which were nice for most of the time? One or two might not be nice at all, but might just be putting it on for the party. And very sorry he would be if he married one of them! Prince Bennett's head was spinning by the time he came and sat down beside Florizella, who was just finishing a bowl of raspberries.

'Would you like a dance?' he asked politely.

'Not especially,' said Florizella. 'And I would have thought you might have had enough.'

'Yes, I have,' Prince Bennett said honestly. 'I think it's the worst party I've ever been to.'

'Have a choc-ice,' said Florizella to cheer him up, and Prince Bennett started to feel better.

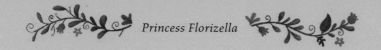

'You're a girl,' he said trustingly. 'You advise me. How can you tell which princesses are really nice and which are just pretending?'

Florizella looked around. 'I only know a few of them. Most of them I don't know any better than you do,' she said. 'The thing you have to remember is that they all have to be nice to you because it's in the Rules. You're the handsome prince.'

'That's just it!' Bennett groaned. 'How do I choose which one to marry?'

'You could disguise yourself as a woodcutter,' Florizella said helpfully, 'and go away for seven years, walk all round other kingdoms and see if you meet your True Love.'

'That's a really rubbish idea,' Prince Bennett said. 'I'm not cutting wood for seven years.'

'Or you could go and work as a swineherd in a royal palace and see if the princess chooses you?'

'I'm not being a swineherd!' Bennett exclaimed. 'Do you have any idea what swine are?'

'Then don't marry anyone,' Florizella said helpfully. 'I wouldn't.'

'But I have to! All princes have to give balls and choose their princess and get married. Then they have to live happily ever after.'

Florizella frowned. 'I know people say that's a happy ending, but they never say exactly how to do it.'

Prince Bennett nodded. 'Or how to do it forever after,' he said dolefully. 'That's the whole problem with being a fairytale prince.'

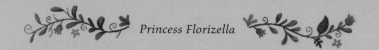

Then the band played and poor Prince Bennett had to go and dance with another princess, and then another and another, until the clock struck midnight and all the princesses got up at once, rushed up the stairs and limped to their beds. There were one hundred and twenty glass slippers dumped on the stairs like a jumble sale. Bennett picked up sixty of them, and then gave up.

'This is getting completely ridiculous,' said Florizella.

CHAPTER THREE

*The morning after –
everyone has to find
their own shoes*

That night all the beautiful princesses set their alarm clocks for six in the morning to give themselves time to get up early and find their shoes, have their baths, wash their hair and put on new dresses for breakfast.

The next day, Prince Bennett was in the parlour waiting for them, and as each princess

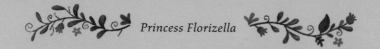

came in, he bowed very low and said, 'Good morning!'

Each princess curtsied and smiled, and said, 'Good morning, Prince Bennett!'

Then the tired prince said, 'What would you like for breakfast?'

And each princess said, 'I don't know. What are *you* having?'

When Prince Bennett said he was having porridge, every one of the one hundred and twenty princesses gasped as if he had said something dreadful, and said, 'Oh, no! Not for me! Just a glass of herbal tea, please! Nothing else!'

One or two of them even said, 'Just a glass of hot water!' and all the other princesses looked envious that they had not thought of

that, and gazed at Prince Bennett to see if he was impressed.

So he was very glad to see Princess Florizella, who came in late because she had been out to the stables to see her horse. And he was very glad when she said at once that she would like bacon and eggs, and tomatoes and sausages too, if they had any. They had a most peaceful, hearty breakfast while, all around, the one hundred and twenty princesses sipped tea and looked beautiful but hungry.

After breakfast, Prince Bennett asked the princess on his right what she would like to do that day. And the princess on his right said, 'I don't know. What would *you* like to do?'

Then Prince Bennett asked the princess on his left what she would like to do that day. And

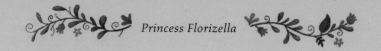

she said, 'I don't know. What would *you* like to do?'

Then Princess Florizella suggested very helpfully, 'Why don't we all ride down to the Deep Lakes and go swimming? We could take a picnic with us.'

Well – some of the princesses couldn't ride, and some of them couldn't swim. Some of them hadn't got trousers for riding, and some of them hadn't got swimming costumes. Some of them were frightened of cold water, and some of them were frightened of horses, and none of them would dream of eating a picnic sitting on the ground where there might be ants or wasps.

'Or grass!' one of them exclaimed.

And they all said, 'Grass stains! Oh no!'

So in the end, no one went ... except Princess Florizella and Prince Bennett.

They had a lovely day.

When they were trotting back to the prince's palace in the evening, just as the stars were starting to come out and the sky was getting grey, Prince Bennett said happily, 'Florizella, I've had the most brilliant idea. I won't marry any of the one hundred and twenty beautiful princesses. I'll marry you!'

And then Florizella said something that surprised him so much that he nearly fell off his horse.

'No, thank you,' she said politely.

Prince Bennett gawped at her. 'Why ever

not?' he asked. 'I am a fairytale prince, remember. And you would be my queen.'

'Look here,' said Florizella reasonably, 'I told you I wasn't going to marry, and I meant it. One day I shall inherit the Seven Kingdoms, and there are a lot of things I want to do there. I don't want to come and be your queen. I'm not even sure that I think kings and queens are a good idea. It might be a lot better for everyone if people made up their own laws and didn't have one person ruling everything.

'Why should I come and live in your palace when I've got a perfectly good palace of my own? I'm not even planning to keep that one all to myself – I'm going to share it. Another home would just be greedy.

'And I don't want to live in your country. I've

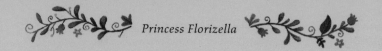

got one of my own. I don't need your fortune. I can earn my own money. I'd very much like it if you were my friend, though – my best friend, if you like. But I don't want to marry you. I'm not actually intending to marry anyone.'

Prince Bennett rode along saying nothing for a little while. He was wondering if he really liked this new sort of princess. Certainly, she wasn't like the normal ones in fairy tales. This was not how the Rules said it should be. Perhaps it was better for him to have a princess at his side who agreed with every single thing he said, however stupid? But then he smiled.

'Florizella,' he said, 'I think I agree with you. I won't choose a princess to marry, either. I shall tell my mother and father. And I should like to be best friends with you.'

So Princess Florizella and Prince Bennett shook hands and rode back side by side in the starlight.

CHAPTER FOUR

*The king becomes a tyrant -
as unfortunately they
so often do*

When Florizella got home, the king and queen were waiting for her at the door of the palace.

'How did you get on?' asked the queen.

'Who did he choose for his bride?' asked the king.

'How many princesses were there at the ball?' asked the queen.

'Did he choose the princess of Three Rivers?' the king asked.

Florizella laughed and jumped out of the carriage.

'I had a lovely time,' she said. 'And he decided not to marry anybody just yet. There were one hundred and twenty princesses there as well as me, and I didn't spot the princess of the Three Rivers, but the place was so awash with princesses that I didn't even see the princess of the Two Mountains, who promised to meet me there.'

'Not choosing a bride!' said the king.

'Not choosing a bride!' said the queen.

Then they both fell on Florizella at once, demanding to know what on earth could have made him decide not to choose a princess at a princess-choosing ball. They were secretly afraid that Florizella had somehow put him off marriage.

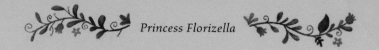

So Florizella explained that Prince Bennett thought the nice princesses might have been just pretending to be nice and might be secretly rather awful to live with, and he hadn't wanted to take the chance.

'Did he ask no one at all, then?' demanded the king. 'Not one of them?'

'Oh yes,' said Florizella. 'He asked me. But I told him I didn't want to marry yet.'

The king and queen stared at each other for a stunned moment, then they both rushed at Florizella again and made her sit down and tell them all about the ball and the breakfast and the horseride and the picnic for two and Prince Bennett asking her to marry him under the stars. They took a lot of interest in the stars. And if there was a nightingale singing. Then

the king jumped to his feet and went to the window and said, 'Undoubtedly! *Undootedly!*' a great many times, very softly.

And the queen had a little smile on her face as she looked at Florizella.

'What a match!' said the king. 'Prince Bennett's kingdom! The Land of Deep Lakes! It's beyond my wildest dreams!'

'What a triumph!' said the queen. 'And everyone always said she was such an *odd* sort of princess!'

Florizella looked from one to the other.

'I said I didn't want to marry him, and we agreed to be just friends,' she said. But she could tell they weren't listening.

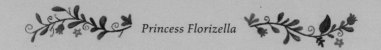

The next day, her father the king laughed and teased her all day, calling her the Queen of the Land of Deep Lakes, which was rather irritating.

The second day, the queen spoke of inviting Prince Bennett over to stay.

The next couple of days there were lots of letters between Prince Bennett's parents and Florizella's mother and father. Then on the fifth day the king told Florizella that she was going to marry Bennett whether she wanted to or not.

Florizella looked at him as if he were crazy. 'You can't make me marry someone if I don't want to,' she said. 'It's just wrong.'

'Oh, can't I?' said the king.

He snatched Florizella up and bundled her

upstairs, and locked her in her bedroom.

'You'll stay there until you agree to marry Prince Bennett!' he bawled through the keyhole.

'Nonsense,' said Florizella. She knew perfectly well that her father had no right to lock her up, or to order her to marry anyone. No one can tell a girl who she has to marry. She also knew that if she wanted to leave, nothing was easier than to open her bedroom window and climb down the drainpipe. After all, she went out like that most mornings to go horseriding. It was so much easier than opening the great double doors, raising the portcullis and lowering the drawbridge on her own. But, instead of running off, she thought she would wait until her father came to let her

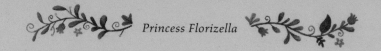

out and talk the whole thing over with him. So she got one of her favourite storybooks and settled down for a quiet morning's reading.

Florizella's lunch was served on a tray in her room by ten footmen.

At teatime they arrived again with a cup of tea and a slice of cake.

By dinnertime Florizella had finished her book and was pretty bored.

At bedtime her father came to the door and said in his most kingly voice, 'My daughter, Princess Florizella, this is your father.'

'I did know that already,' she said.

'Do you agree to marry Prince Bennett?'

Florizella, who was rather sulky, for she

had wasted a whole day indoors while the sun was shining outside, said, 'Certainly not! And you know you shouldn't treat a daughter like this. Not even in a fairy story.'

At that, the king stamped off to bed in a terrible temper. He was cross because Florizella would not do as he wanted, and he was cross because he knew perfectly well he was in the wrong.

'She's acting like she thinks she's a prince!' he complained to the queen as they went to bed that night.

'A princess is just a prince with more s's,' she replied.

The king thought for a moment. 'What do the s's stand for?'

'Sass,' she said. 'Sass and science, sensibility

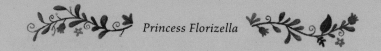

and scepticism. Sincerity, spirit and certainty.'

'That's a *c*,' said the king. 'Undoubtedly.'

'And tomorrow,' the queen continued, 'Florizella is to be let out, whatever she says about Prince Bennett.'

The king said, 'Humph,' as if he meant *No*. But he really meant *Yes*. There is nothing more boring than being a tyrant.

CHAPTER FIVE

*The difficulties
of being different*

ut next morning, before anyone was up, there was a great *Tooroo! Tooroo!* at the palace gates, and in galloped Prince Bennett with half a dozen of his courtiers, a dozen soldiers and a couple of trumpeters. Just a small informal visit.

He had come to see the king, for someone had told him that Princess Florizella was locked in her room and that the king would

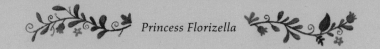

not let her out until she promised to marry the prince.

Prince Bennett popped up to the king's bedroom and argued with him while the king sat up in bed and longed for his morning tea. He had never liked Bennett less than he did at that moment.

Just think of him married to Florizella and living in the palace! the king warned himself. *I'd never have a peaceful morning.*

But, out loud, all he said was that Prince Bennett should go home and wait for a message, and that he was certain Florizella would agree to a wedding soon. And then the footmen finally poured the morning cup of tea, and the king looked so hard at the door and at Prince Bennett and back again,

that even the prince could see he was very much in the way. So he made a bow and got himself out of the room as quickly as he could go backwards. (You're not supposed to turn your back on the royals. It's a nuisance when you're in a hurry.)

Prince Bennett didn't go home, of course. He at least knew how a prince should behave in a crisis. He popped round to the back of the castle and hooted like an owl until Princess Florizella put her head out of the window and said, 'Don't be silly, Bennett. Everyone knows owls come out at night. Besides, that wasn't anything like an owl.'

Then they argued about whether or not owls made calls like *too-wit-too-whoo*, or whether it was more like *hoo-hee, hoo-hoo*, and whether

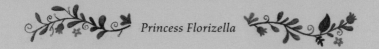

they came out at dawn or dusk. They made owl calls at each other until all the windows of the castle opened and lots of people put their heads out to see what was going on.

'What on earth is that racket?' the queen asked her maid, pausing in the middle of trying on one of her twenty crowns.

'Princess Florizella's young prince, Your Majesty, making secret signals to her,' said the maid, leaning out of the window to have a good look.

'He's come to rescue her, then,' said the queen, extremely pleased. 'That's very prompt. I like a young man who gets on with a rescue.

When I was a princess, my future husband, the dear king, was very late. I was tied to a rock for three days, and if the sea monster had not had an upset stomach, my dear husband might have been too late altogether. It's not all fun being a princess, you know.'

The maid nodded and looked out of the window again.

'He's climbing up to her bedroom, ma'am,' she said.

'That's unusual,' said the queen, with interest. 'I'd have thought Florizella would have had the sheets knotted together by now. How is he climbing? Not by her hair – it's not nearly long enough. She *will* keep having it cut. I *told* her she'd need it one of these days.'

'Up the ivy, ma'am,' said the maid. 'Looks

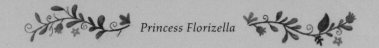

a bit unsteady to me.'

The queen smiled because it had been her idea to plant the ivy outside Princess Florizella's bedroom on the very morning that she was born, to be ready for just such an occasion. And now here was Prince Bennett climbing up it to free Florizella! It was very gratifying. Next, Bennett would rescue Florizella and ride away with her. Then the queen and the king could forgive them and they could all have a wonderful party and live happily ever after.

But she should have remembered that Florizella was not like other princesses.

Prince Bennett should have remembered that Florizella was not like other princesses.

She was not a bit grateful to him for climbing up the ivy.

'But I've come to rescue you!' Bennett protested, scrambling through the window and diving head-first on to the floor.

'How did you get to my bedroom window?' she demanded as if she had not seen him scrambling, and grabbing for the drainpipe when a branch broke.

'The ivy,' Bennett said, surprised at the question.

'And don't you think,' said Florizella sarcastically, 'that if *you* can climb up, then *I* can perfectly well climb down?'

Bennett said nothing. He hadn't thought of that. He was so used to the old idea of princesses sitting still and waiting to be rescued that he had forgotten Florizella did not follow the Princess Rules.

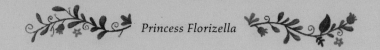

'Just go,' said Florizella, giving him a little push towards the window. 'It's bad enough with everyone nagging me to marry you, without you carrying on like a prince in an old fairy story as well.'

'But what about you?' Bennett asked, rather worried.

Florizella laughed. 'My father will let me out soon enough,' she said. 'And, if I get too bored, I can always climb down the drainpipe and go for a ride. When I'm out, I'll come over and see you. But I'll stay here for now. My father shouldn't have locked me in, and I want to talk to him about it. He'll never learn to treat girls properly unless I tell him.'

Bennett thought that perhaps Florizella was not a very comfortable daughter for anyone to

have. And he thought that perhaps she would not be a very obedient wife. But she was a great friend. So he shook hands with her and climbed out of the window.

'Gracious me, ma'am!' squawked the queen's maid. 'It's Prince Bennett coming back down the ivy. *On his own!* He's left the princess behind!'

The queen dashed to the window and watched Prince Bennett scramble down, whistle for his horse, mount up, signal to his trumpeters to go *Tooroo! Tooroo!* and gallop off without a care in the world and – more importantly – without a rescued princess across his saddlebow.

'Oh no!' she said. She had no doubt who was to blame. 'Oh no! *Oh, Florizella!*'

CHAPTER SIX

*The benefits of
being different*

When the king heard what had happened, he went bananas.

There was no chance that he was going to let Florizella out now. He had been so sure that Bennett was going to rescue her, he was even prepared to overlook the way the prince had bothered him so early in the morning. But for the prince to leave without taking Princess Florizella with him, breaking all the traditions

of fairy stories and happy endings!

'*Amateur!*' he snapped and stumped off to the garden to prune the roses. 'Half-hearted,' he said with a snip. 'Half-witted, more like,' he said, taking off another flower.

There wasn't a single rose blooming by lunchtime, but the king was feeling a lot better.

Until the messenger came, that is.

It was one of Prince Bennett's trumpeters. She came *Tooroo, Tooroo*ing into the courtyard in a terrible hurry, scaring the hens half to death and setting the guard dogs barking.

'Prince Bennett has been captured!' she shouted. 'He was on his way home when he was captured by a dragon in the Purple Forest!'

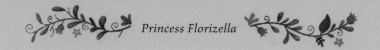

Everyone came running at once. Florizella opened her window to listen. The messenger told them that the great two-headed dragon of the Purple Forest had jumped out at the prince and his courtiers, and everyone had ridden away as fast as they could except for Prince Bennett, whose horse reared and dropped him right at the dragon's feet. Bennett had bent his sword in the fall and couldn't draw it from the scabbard! As he lay there, stunned and helpless ('Amateur!' the king exclaimed. 'As I said. Nincompoop!'), the dragon had picked him up and tied him to a tree, using all sorts of particularly difficult knots, and was sitting beside him, waiting for forty-eight hours (according to Dragon Association Rules) for the rescue party to arrive, before

eating the prince up – every little bit of him except, possibly, the bent sword.

'Ooo!' said Florizella, privately rather pleased at hearing this, and she leaned out of the window and whistled a loud, clear whistle that Jellybean could hear wherever he happened to be. He was in his stable and had to back up against the far wall and take a little run at the door and rear up to jump over it, and then he came galloping round and crashed to a stop under Florizella's window. Florizella grabbed her sword and her dagger, and a spare sword for Prince Bennett (which she kept in the wardrobe in the space for the long dresses) and shinned down the drainpipe as quickly as she could.

She dropped on to Jellybean's back and

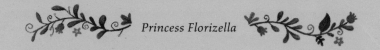

galloped as fast as she could to the Purple Forest, steering Jellybean with the halter rope and clinging on tightly to the two swords.

She saw the dragon before he saw her.

He had dozed off while he was waiting, with an alarm clock in one of his great green ears to wake him when the forty-eight hours were up. His snores bent the tallest trees of the Purple Forest and made a noise like a thousand thunderstorms. His reeking, smoky breath scorched all the grass and flowers and bushes for three miles around, so that Jellybean snorted and shivered at the dreadful smell of burning.

Bennett was tied to a tree with fiendishly complicated dragon knots, looking rather white and scared. But as soon as he saw

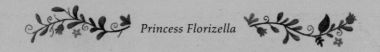
Florizella, he whispered as softly as he could, 'Florizella! Untie me, quick!'

Florizella had a look at the knots as she jumped out of the saddle and thought it would take her all of the forty-eight hours to get even one of them undone and, drawing her sharp sword, she cut through the rope. She and Bennett were just about to get up on Jellybean and gallop away, when . . .

. . . the dragon woke up!

CHAPTER SEVEN

*Why it's good that there
is more than one way
to be a princess*

As soon as the dragon saw Florizella and Bennett, he let out a dreadful great roar. His yellow eyes flashed and smoke spouted from all his nostrils in both his noses.

Florizella and Bennett stood back to back without saying a word, and both drew their swords. The dragon lurched towards them, his two great scaly heads getting closer and closer.

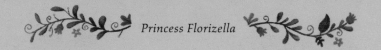

Florizella's sword went up, and Bennett's too, and before the dragon had a chance to blow flaming breath all over them, the two heroes brought their swords down with a mighty *swoosh* and a horrid *thwack* that resounded through the forest.

The dragon lay dead at their feet, disappearing from its toes up, as dragons do when their heads are cut off, and *That was the End of Him.*

'Wow!' said Bennett. They both leaned down and wiped the blades of their weapons on the grass and the ferns of the forest. Their swords were smeared with the dragon's bright-green blood. It made them both feel a bit sick just to see it. When their swords were clean, they gave each other a hug and

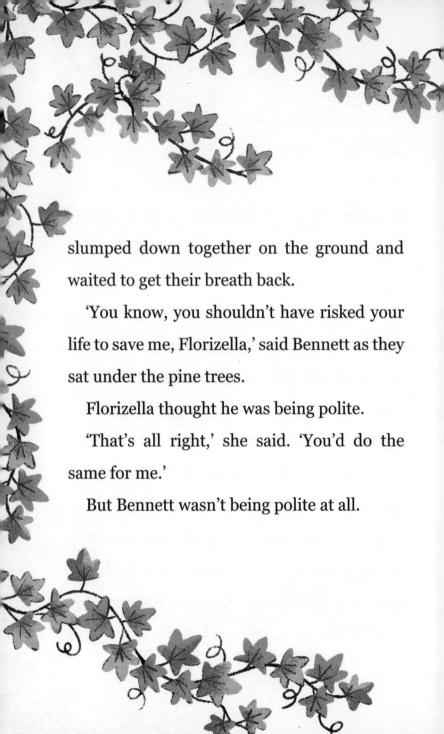

slumped down together on the ground and waited to get their breath back.

'You know, you shouldn't have risked your life to save me, Florizella,' said Bennett as they sat under the pine trees.

Florizella thought he was being polite.

'That's all right,' she said. 'You'd do the same for me.'

But Bennett wasn't being polite at all.

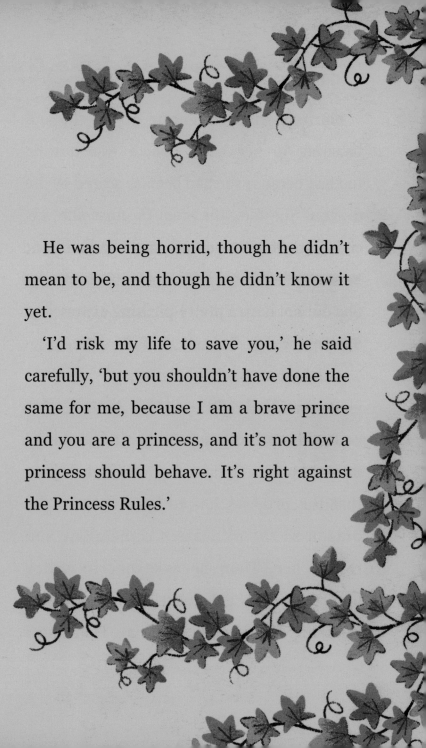

He was being horrid, though he didn't mean to be, and though he didn't know it yet.

'I'd risk my life to save you,' he said carefully, 'but you shouldn't have done the same for me, because I am a brave prince and you are a princess, and it's not how a princess should behave. It's right against the Princess Rules.'

Florizella stopped staring at the sky and listening to her heart, which was beating too fast because she had been so scared by the dragon. She took the stem of grass she was chewing out of her mouth and she looked at Bennett. She did not look at him affectionately. She did not have a pretty-pleasing expression. She squinted at Bennett as if she thought he was about to say something stupid.

She was dead right.

'It's the prince's job to do the rescuing,' Bennett prince-splained. 'Everybody knows that the princess has to be caught by the dragon so the prince can come along and rescue her. Then he asks her to marry him and they get married to universal rejoicing. Everyone knows that. That's how

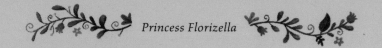

we should have done it.'

'There wouldn't be universal rejoicing if we got married,' Florizella said sharply. 'Because one person, at least, wouldn't be rejoicing, and that would be me. You know very well that I don't want to get married yet. You know very well that we agreed to be friends. And if you want to be friends with me then you have to see that I am not the sort of princess who is going to get caught by a dragon and wait to be rescued!'

She jumped up and whistled for Jellybean, collecting the cut ropes and gathering the swords in a very busy, cross way.

'But that's how princes and princesses are supposed to be!' said Prince Bennett, a bit cross himself. 'We're supposed to warn you, you're

supposed to wander into obvious danger, then I am supposed to rescue you.'

Florizella put a hand on Jellybean's halter and looked at the prince with blazing eyes.

'Suit yourself!' she said crossly. 'If you want to be best friends, then you come to me when I need you and I'll come to you when you need me. But if you want to be like other princes and princesses and get married as soon as something interesting happens, so that nothing interesting ever happens again, that's up to you! But I told you once and I'll tell you again – I *won't* get married for a good long while. And I *won't* marry you just because we fought a dragon together. You said we were best friends, and that's what I want. But if you want me to be a regular

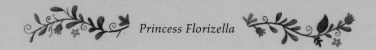

princess – and worse than that – a princess who has to be rescued, then you can fight your own dragons . . . and I hope they eat you!'

'But a proper princess—' Bennett started.

'This is a proper princess,' Florizella yelled, waving her sword above her head in her agitation. '*I am a proper princess!* Like a prince only with more *s*'s!'

'Why, what do the *s*'s stand for?'

'Swordsmanship,' said Florizella crushingly, and she jumped on Jellybean, dug her heels in and scorched off at a gallop. She did not even look back at poor Prince Bennett, standing all alone in the Purple Forest with his broken sword and the trees quietly smouldering all around him.

She went home, put Jellybean back in his stall and gave him a rub-down and a feed. Then she climbed up the drainpipe (for her bedroom door was still locked) and pulled back the covers on her bed, tumbled in and fell fast asleep. She was very tired.

So she did not know until the next morning that she and Bennett were the best of friends after all. For when the rescue party finally

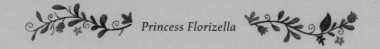

arrived in the Purple Forest, he did not go straight home, where his parents were anxiously waiting. He rode all the way back to Florizella's kingdom and, for the second time that day, he sought and found the king, Florizella's father, and addressed him as 'Sire' just like a proper fairy tale.

Bennett told the king straight that he would never marry Florizella, unless one day she really wanted to marry him.

'And I think, Sire,' he said, 'that a girl who is big enough to kill her own dragon is big enough to make up her own mind.'

The king could not help but agree and give Prince Bennett a hug.

'Undoubtedly! *Undootedly!*' he said.

And the queen, who had taught Florizella

sword-fighting in the first place, nodded rather proudly and said, 'Well, Florizella was never just an *ordinary* princess.'

She hugged Prince Bennett too, and they sent him home in the second-best royal carriage, the silver one with the blue cushions. And from that day onwards no one *ever* suggested that Princess Florizella should obey the Princess Rules.

Least of all Prince Bennett.

Florizella and the Wolves

CHAPTER ONE

*Princess Florizella sets out for
a lovely ride on a fine day.
What could possibly go wrong?*

It was a bright, sunny morning as Princess Florizella threw back her bedroom curtains and saw, to her relief, that no overnight spell had turned her kingdom into a watery waste, or the people into butterflies, or any of the other tedious and unpredictable things that can happen to a fairytale princess.

Since everything seemed normal, she leaned out of the window to see her horse, Jellybean,

grazing in the field beyond the palace gardens. She put two fingers in her mouth and gave a piercing whistle. Jellybean's head went up and his ears went forward and he thundered down the paddock towards the gate and cleared it with a metre to spare, narrowly missing the king, who was gardening on the other side.

'I do wish she wouldn't do that,' said the king as he pulled himself out of the rose bush.

The queen gave him a helpful tug, and watched Florizella slide down the drainpipe and jump from the windowsill on to Jellybean's warm back, and trot round to the stables.

'I wish she'd use the doors,' she agreed. 'But she's always been a princess in her own way.'

'Undoubtedly!' said the king, with much feeling. '*Undootedly!*'

Florizella had Jellybean tacked up in a few minutes. She put on her hard hat with its smart princess cover, and trotted out of the stableyard, over the castle drawbridge and down the lane towards the Purple Forest.

It was a wonderful day in early summer; the scarlet swallows and the golden swifts were swooping low over the river, and in the central square, the fairies were holding a farmers' market, buying and selling farmers. Florizella was singing to herself, and Jellybean put his ears forward and went into an easy canter down the track that runs through the Purple Forest and up to the high moorland.

But somehow they took a wrong turn.

Florizella rode for a little while, then she pulled Jellybean to a standstill and looked

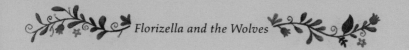

around. She had never been this deep into the Purple Forest before and she was surprised at how dark it was. She knew there were wolves and lions in the forest, as well as witches and enchanters. Florizella felt rather uncomfortable – as if there were cold fingers walking up and down her spine.

It grew darker, and Florizella started to wish she was at home. The black bushes and shadowy trees seemed to whisper in the wind, and the little rustlings sounded like someone coming closer.

Jellybean put back his ears, a sure sign that he was unhappy, and moved restlessly. Florizella patted his neck and said, 'Silly Jellybean! Fancy being frightened!' as if she were not nervous herself, and she turned

him round to ride back the way she had come.

Then suddenly the rain started – great thick drops of rain that cascaded through the leaves of the trees and soaked Florizella and Jellybean in seconds so they both stopped being scared and became cold and miserable. Jellybean's head drooped and his lovely bright chestnut coat went all streaky and dark with the wet. Florizella was wet through, rain dripping off her hat and down her neck.

Then there was a great *Crash!* of thunder and a great *Crack-crack!* of lightning. Jellybean flung up his head and reared in fright and Florizella tumbled off his back and down into the mud. Before she could catch the reins, Jellybean was gone! Back to his warm stable –

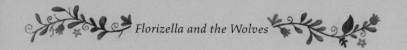

because he had known the way home all along, but hadn't been able to explain it.

That was bad. But there was worse to come!

The lightning had struck a great tree nearby – it was groaning and creaking and swaying. Florizella could see it looming over her, but she was so stunned by her fall that she couldn't move. She could only lie there in the mud while the great tree leaned and cracked and finally came down with a great roar and a crackle of breaking branches.

She was always the *luckiest* of princesses! The two main branches of the tree fell either side of her. The tree trunk, which could have crushed her, fell short; the boughs that could have broken her bones were spread out all around her.

'Crikey!' said Florizella when she dared to open her eyes.

The storm was still raging, and as she struggled to sit up and look through the great bushy branches of leaves, she heard the thunder roll again, and the lightning was as bright as fireworks. Florizella heard another tree crashing down, and she knew that she had to find shelter. She scrambled over the branches and looked around in the stormy darkness.

There was a little hill to her left, away from the path, and some solid-looking boulders. Florizella thought that if she could creep under one of the rocks she would be out of the rain and safe from any more falling trees. She scrambled up the hill, her path sometimes very

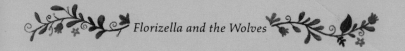

bright from lightning and sometimes very black from the storm; her eyes sometimes able to see everything as clear as day for the few seconds of light, and then quite blind afterwards. The rain poured down on her, and she was wet through and gasping – it was like being under a super-strong power shower turned to COLD – but eventually she scrambled up the slope and reached the top of the hill and found, to her relief, a proper cave.

CHAPTER TWO

*Florizella finds safety
but has rather a horrid
feeling about it*

he entrance to the cave was a little patch of grass and one rock leaning against another to make a doorway. Florizella dropped to her hands and knees and squeezed through. The roof of the cave was higher inside and Florizella was able to stand up and feel her way along the wall towards the back. She sat down in the darkness and thought that she

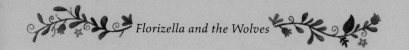

was lucky to be safe and out of the rain.

Then she stopped feeling lucky, and felt instead . . . a Horrid Feeling.

It is the feeling you get when you think you are in a room on your own, and you suddenly know that someone else is there.

That sort of Horrid Feeling.

It is the feeling you get when you play games like What's the Time, Mister Wolf? or Cat and Mouse, or Grandmother's Footsteps, when you turn your back, and the other people creep quietly, quietly up on you.

You don't need to turn round to see your friends coming closer and closer in those games. You can *feel* them sneaking up.

It was that kind of feeling for Florizella.

She knew that she was not alone in the cave.

She knew that there was something else in the cave too. She knew it was sneaking up on her.

As she stayed very still and listened, she could hear it breathing.

She was scared then, all right.

Prince with two *s*'s or not, brave or not, Florizella was very scared then. She could clearly hear soft little breaths. And, what was worse, they were coming from between her and the entrance. Whatever was sharing the cave with her and gently panting, had her trapped. And she did not have a clue what it might be.

Florizella froze as still as a statue and listened as hard as she could. Nothing happened for long, scary moments. The princess put her back to the cave wall and looked around in the

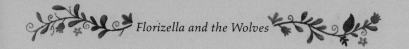

darkness, straining her eyes to see.

Then she felt something extremely soft touch her foot.

She very nearly screamed and jumped, but she did not. You might hope this was because she was a brave princess who feared nothing! You might hope that she remembered the Princess Rule, which says that a princess never raises her voice except in the case of fire. But that is not true either. She did not scream and jump, she did not run away, because she was frightened rigid. She let out a tiny little mouse-squeak and stayed as still as a stone princess.

Then she heard a funny little growl and a scuffle, and something warm and heavy tumbled over her other foot.

So there were two of IT.

And they were small.

And they were light, Florizella thought, *as light as . . . puppies.* They were puppy-shaped, they made little puppyish noises, they smelled that delicious smell of warm, dry fur and clean paws, and they were playing in the dark with each other.

Florizella laughed out loud and put her hand down to her feet to feel for them. As her eyes got used to the darkness she could just see them. One, two, three, four darling little puppies with smooth grey coats and fat little bellies and big black eyes, tumbling over each other and biting each other's tails and paws. Florizella sat down among them and picked them up and put them on her lap.

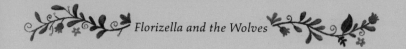

They were adorable. They tumbled on to the floor and they bit the belt on her trousers. They gnawed at the heels of her riding boots, made fierce little attacks on her twiddling fingers, and climbed all over her.

Florizella thought that they must belong to a couple of dogs lost by their owners in the forest, or perhaps a dog that had run away from home to have puppies on her own. But she didn't think much about the mother dog at all.

And that was a mistake. A very big mistake.

Florizella sat on the floor of the cave and played with the puppies as if she were a young silly puppy herself. She didn't think about the mother dog or the father dog once.

Until . . .

The entrance to the cave suddenly grew dark as the light was blocked by a great animal coming in. A great animal coming back into its own cave, to feed its young. A huge animal, so big that it had to squeeze in through the cave mouth. It smelled Florizella the moment it was inside, and it looked for her with its fierce orange eyes, and then it growled.

And Florizella, silly Florizella, looked up from playing with the puppies and saw the light blocked by the great animal and saw . . . not a lost pet dog . . . but a *wolf*.

Worse than that (twice as bad, to be very precise) she saw *two wolves*. The mother and the father wolf came into the cave and glared at Florizella sitting on the floor of their cave

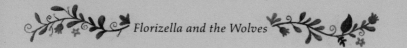

with their puppies on her knees.

Florizella stayed very still. She had no weapon and, anyway, she couldn't fight two wolves at once. No one was going to rescue her as no one knew where she was. If she were going to get out of this adventure alive, she would have to do it all on her own, with skill, and a lot of luck.

'Nice wolves,' said Florizella nervously into the darkness. 'Here are your puppies. See? I was just petting them.' Carefully she put them on the floor and they stumbled on their fat feet over to their parents. The mother wolf dropped to the ground with a dead rabbit in her mouth and tore off little bits of meat and skin for the puppies. The father wolf sat on his haunches to guard them and looked at

Florizella with his marmalade-coloured eyes. He didn't take his gaze off her once. He didn't even blink.

Florizella sat very still and waited for them to finish their meal. Overall, she thought it was better if they were not hungry. Being stuck in a cave with six wolves is dangerous – six hungry wolves is worse. She didn't say a word, but she couldn't help shivering. She shivered so hard that her teeth chattered like clattering castanets. The mother wolf glanced up at the noise. Florizella gritted her teeth and tried to shiver in silence.

When the puppies had played and pulled at the meat, and eaten a little, the mother wolf sprawled out and they swarmed up to her belly and sucked milk from her. The smell of wet

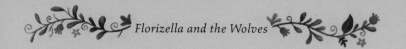

wolf filled the cave, and the noise was rather soothing. The cave was small and, when the mother wolf stretched out, her head rested on Florizella's foot. Florizella froze, not daring to move, but the mother wolf took no notice of anything but her four wolf cubs sucking like little pumps and wagging their tails. The father wolf picked his way over them and sat down opposite Florizella, watching her with his unwinking amber eyes.

Florizella stayed as still as she could, waiting for him to pounce.

But he did not pounce. Instead, he turned round and round two or three times like the palace pet dog in his basket, and then he lay down beside her. Soon he was breathing steadily and Florizella could tell he was asleep.

Now the cave was very quiet. The father wolf, stretched out to his full length alongside Florizella's leg, made her feel warmer. All four cubs were well fed and dreaming – Florizella could hear them snoring softly through milky whiskers. The mother wolf's head rested, warm and heavy, on Florizella's foot.

With one warm, heavy wolf on one foot, and another warm wolf stretched along her leg, Florizella wasn't cold any more. She felt quite cosy – a bit nervous maybe – but no longer chilled. She thought she would wait a moment till they were deeply asleep and then creep out of the cave. She leaned back against the wall and closed her eyes for a few moments.

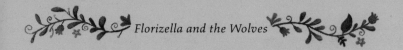

And then it was Florizella who fell deeply asleep.

The four wolf cubs, the mother and father wolf and Princess Florizella slept sweetly until morning.

CHAPTER THREE

*Florizella eats
a varied diet*

here was uproar in the palace when
Jellybean galloped in with his reins
loose, and the stirrups flapping, and no Florizella.
There were search parties in all directions
and diviners with wands. They were all very
relieved when Florizella walked in the next
morning, damp and rather smelly, and told
them all about her night in the wolves' cave.
Then she begged the king and queen to outlaw

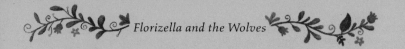

wolf-hunting for the season, so that the four little wolf cubs could grow up safely in the Purple Forest. And Florizella's mother and father – who believed in magic and in paying debts – agreed that their daughter had been spared by the wolves, so the least they could do was to make sure that all wolves were safe for a season.

Throughout the land of the Seven Kingdoms everyone was warned that wolf-hunting was illegal for the rest of the year. All the wolves – including the quite beastly ones – enjoyed a pleasant holiday eating other people's goats, popping into hen houses and howling at the full moon.

One day Princess Florizella was in the courtyard feeding the golden carp in the fountain pond when a trader rode into the castle yard. He was very red-faced and hot because he wore or carried all his stock. He was wearing three shirts, two jackets and four capes. His poor horse was quite bow-legged under the weight of the saddle packs. He had toys in the right-side pack, and books in the left. He had bolts of cloth strapped on the back of the saddle, a carpet rolled up in front – and spread out over the horse's hindquarters . . . he had a pair of beautiful fresh wolfskins.

As soon as Florizella saw them, she let out a shriek and raced up to him and grabbed his stirrup leather.

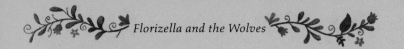

'*Where did you hunt those wolves?*' she demanded, so fiercely that the man was quite afraid.

'In the Purple Forest,' he said, looking over her head to the grooms. One of them made a warning face at him, but he had travelled so far, and for so long, that he did not know this girl was Princess Florizella, and he did not know about the ban on wolf-hunting.

'How could you!' said Florizella, nearly crying. 'Was it a male and a female?'

'Yes, a pair,' he said. 'I trapped them by a tree that had been struck by lightning, just beside the track.'

Florizella looked at him as if he were worse than a slug.

'That's forbidden!' she said furiously.

'There was to be no hunting of wolves this season to protect a special family of wolves. They lived in a cave near that tree. I think you've killed them!'

The trader stammered that he had not known about the ban on wolf-hunting, but Florizella looked at him as if he were worse than a slug: a squashed slug, an old, dried-out squashed slug, until he stopped and shrugged his shoulders, and said there was nothing he could do about it. For the wolves were dead and that was the end of it.

It wasn't the end as far as Florizella was concerned.

She felt that she owed the wolves a debt of gratitude. They could have attacked her, but instead they had shared their cave with her.

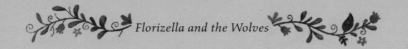

They could have eaten her up, but instead they had kept her warm.

So, while the trader was in the castle apologising to the king and queen, Florizella went to the kitchen and fetched a strong basket, lined it with a soft tea towel (which she took without asking!), whistled for Jellybean and set off for the Purple Forest.

Why did she need the strong basket and the soft tea towel?

Wait and see.

Florizella had no difficulty in finding the track, and as soon as she came to the tree that had been struck by lightning she tied Jellybean to one of the fallen branches and

set off up the little hill.

Outside the wolves' cave she stopped and called softly. If they were still alive she didn't really want to meet them again. She wasn't altogether sure that they would be so hospitable on a second visit.

But there was no noise from the cave except a very soft whimpering, which sounded like cubs.

It sounded like four very hungry cubs.

Florizella forgot all about being careful and plunged into the narrow entrance of the cave, blinking so that she could see in the gloom.

Four little wolf cubs came squirming up and climbed all over her riding boots. Florizella bent down and stroked them. To

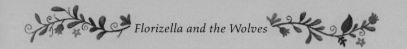

her horror they were not fat little creatures any more. They were thin, so thin that she could feel their sharp little ribs and the bony knobbly bits on their spines. They had not been fed for several days.

Florizella put down the basket and, one by one, lifted the skinny, squirming cubs into it. (That was what the basket was for!) When she picked it up, it was surprisingly heavy. She carried it carefully down the hill to where Jellybean was waiting.

Jellybean didn't really like carrying a basket of wolves, but he went as steady as a rock all the way back to the castle, because he knew that Florizella had only one hand on the reins. And Florizella was lucky when she got home for there was no one in the

courtyard, and no one on the stairs. She got the basket with the cubs in it all the way up to her room, and no one spotted her.

Then she went straight downstairs to the kitchen and told the cook that she was starving hungry.

'You can have a slice of pie,' he said, pointing to the larder. 'There's a nice steak-and-mushroom pie left over from lunch. Or I'm just about to take a chocolate cake out of the oven.'

'I'll have some pie, please,' said Florizella, and the cook was surprised because Florizella adored chocolate cake, but was usually a bit so-so about steak and mushroom.

Florizella slipped into the larder and took the whole pie – a massive great round one.

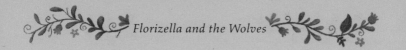

She carried it carefully up to her room and cut it into four portions and put each slice on the floor. The little wolf cubs fell on it like mad things, and in an amazingly short time the pie had gone and there were four little cubs, with bellies as tight as drums, snoozing on the carpet.

Florizella fetched a shawl from a drawer and tucked them up under her bed where they would not be noticed, and went down to her supper.

When Florizella came back from supper, she discovered that keeping wolf cubs is no easy job.

Keeping wolf cubs in secret is impossible.

They had made horrid smelly poos all over the floor, which she had to clean up with paper and a bowl of water. They had hunted her bedcover and pulled it to the floor and killed it. One of them had bitten and swung on the curtains, dragging them right off the pole. And worse than all of that . . . they were hungry again!

As soon as they saw Florizella, they scrambled all over her, making pitiful whines, begging for more food. Florizella looked down at them like a distracted mother and said, 'But you've only *just* been fed!'

The cubs didn't care. There is a reason why people say, 'I am as hungry as a wolf,' and Florizella understood it now. These cubs were wolves and they specialised in being hungry.

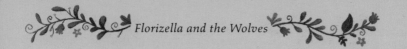

All the time.

Florizella scowled at them. She knew she would have to go back down to the kitchen. And she was wondering if the cook might not find it a bit odd.

He did.

He found it very odd indeed that Princess Florizella should have taken a massive steak-and-mushroom pie up to her room before her supper. He found it very odd that she should have brought the pie dish back quite empty. Then she had eaten a good supper – and one of the footmen had seen her sneak the chop bones off her plate into her pocket.

Now, less than an hour later, Florizella was in the kitchen again, asking for something to eat.

The cook looked at her suspiciously.

'I have chocolate ice cream,' he said. 'Or cheesecake.'

Florizella adored cheesecake. She didn't mind chocolate ice cream, either.

'Do you have any meat?' she asked. 'Any of those chops left over from supper?'

'I have twelve chops,' he said, 'but they're not cooked.'

'Oh, that's all right!' said Florizella hastily, thinking of the hungry little wolf cubs upstairs who would *love* raw lamb chops. 'Even better!'

And to the cook's utter amazement, Florizella went to the larder and came out with a bowl of uncooked lamb chops, and took them to her room as if she had been having

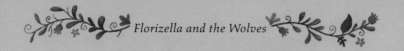

midnight feasts of raw meat all her life.

The cook had an idea.

But he didn't say anything yet.

CHAPTER FOUR

*Bennett comes to the rescue.
No, he really does...*

*N*ext morning when the cook came down to make breakfast, he found that a great haunch of venison had gone. It had been hanging in the larder and it would have been venison pie for thirty people that evening. One of the maids had seen Princess Florizella taking it upstairs.

The cook went to find the king and queen.

'I am sorry to have to tell you, but I am

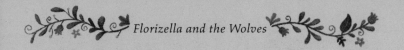

afraid that Princess Florizella is under a lion enchantment,' he said as soon as he was in the royal breakfast parlour.

'In the past twenty-four hours, she has taken from my larder: a steak-and-mushroom pie, a dozen raw lamb chops and a haunch of venison that would have served thirty people.'

The king and queen gasped.

'What's a lion enchantment?' asked the king.

'Someone has put her under a spell to turn her into a lion,' the queen explained. 'But surely it can't be true! Who would do such a thing to Florizella? She's always been so popular, except for that unfortunate incident with a python.'

'Send for the royal enchanter!' said the king. 'This is his sort of thing.'

(In the Seven Kingdoms you can send for an enchanter like you can send for a plumber or an electrician in our world. They have magic there, but no electricity. (Which would you rather have?) It's great for spells, but a nuisance when it's dark, and of course there's no TV, no phones or drones, not even vacuum cleaners or electric toothbrushes. But there are magicians. The royal palace always has two enchanters on call, day and night, in case of visits from wicked fairy godmothers, accidents with spinning wheels, the disappearance of girls or the arrival of armies of gnomes – the sort of things that happen in fairy tales and are *very* inconvenient.)

The royal enchanter came at once, looking grave.

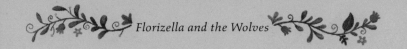

'Eating meat to excess,' he said thoughtfully. 'How does she smell?'

The queen thought hard. Florizella had popped into her room that morning, and after a night with four wolf cubs she had smelled a bit . . . a bit . . .

'Whiffy!' she said honestly.

The enchanter nodded. 'Any sign of a mane growing round her neck and head?' he asked.

The queen looked horrified. What with hiding the venison bone and mopping up after the wolf cubs, Florizella had not bothered to brush her hair that morning. It didn't look in the least like a lion's mane – but frightened people often get things wrong.

'Oh dear!' the queen said. 'And her nails!'

She meant that they were so dirty – Florizella

had torn up the venison into little pieces for the wolf cubs by hand, and she hadn't had time to wash.

'Claws . . .' The enchanter nodded. 'Very bad indeed.'

'Surely not,' the king said quietly.

'Only one solution,' the enchanter announced. 'We'll have to lock her up in her room until we can find who has put this spell on her – and how to lift it.'

'I suppose so—'

'Have to,' the enchanter said briskly. 'Can't have her going around the countryside eating people. Very bad for the monarchy. Nothing upsets people more than a royal family eating small children. The very worst thing that can happen.'

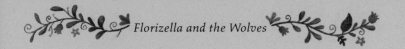

The queen nodded. 'We'll have to keep it secret,' she said. 'I'll order the guards.'

'And I'll tell the cook to keep feeding her meat,' the king said. 'Poor little Florizella, she'll miss her puddings!'

'And I'll cast spells to look for the wizard who has done this,' the royal enchanter promised.

All this time, Florizella was up in her room playing with the wolf cubs, quite forgetting that she was very late for breakfast. She didn't even notice that it was nearly time for lunch.

She did not even hear the key turn as they locked her in. One of the puppies, whom she had named Samson, was hiding under the bed and Florizella was trying to tempt him out by waggling her hairbrush at him. His little furry hackles were raised and he was growling through his tiny white teeth. Then he came out, stalking, just like a grown-up wolf, only ten times smaller. Florizella forgot all about going down to breakfast, and poured them some milk from her morning tea tray.

She was so absorbed she did not hear the tap on the window. Then there was a louder knock. Then there was a hoarse whisper.

'Honestly, Florizella! Are you deaf?'

It was her best friend, Prince Bennett, clinging on to the ivy.

Florizella ran to the window. Samson, the naughty wolf cub, took his chance while her back was turned. He jumped up on to her bed, got under the covers and started tunnelling

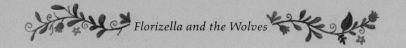
down between the sheets.

'Anybody would think you liked climbing ivy,' Florizella said scornfully as she opened the window and Prince Bennett climbed in. 'What's wrong with the stairs all of a sudden?'

'What's wrong with *you*, you mean!' Bennett said smartly. 'Guards on your door and the place in uproar? Me forbidden to see you – I came over at once, of course.' Then he turned round. 'What was that noise?' he demanded.

Florizella grinned. 'Wolves,' she said.

'No, not a howling from the forest, a kind of scuffling in your bed.'

'Wolves,' said Florizella again, and she pulled back the covers. Bennett saw the little wolf cub blinking at the sunlight, very surprised to find himself on the outside.

'What's this?' said Bennett, amazed. 'What a little darling!' He dropped to his knees to stroke the wolf. At once, two other cubs came tumbling out from underneath the bed. Bennett sat down on the floor and they clambered over him, sniffing and licking and gently nipping him until Bennett forgot all about whispering and roared with laughter.

'What guards on my door?' asked Florizella, taking one of the wolf cubs from out of her bedroom slipper. 'Why aren't you allowed to see me?'

'Oh, that!' Bennett said. 'I understand now. You've been pinching meat from the kitchen to feed this lot, and they all think you have been eating it yourself! You smell dreadfully of wolf, Florizella. And this room is awful!

They've taken it into their heads that you're under a spell and you're turning into a lion, and they've locked you up until they can find the wizard who is doing it to you.'

Florizella shot one amazed look at Bennett. 'Oh no!' She was laughing so much she could hardly speak. 'And I thought I would keep these cubs with no one knowing. And now the whole palace is going crazy.'

'Idiot!' said Bennett lovingly. 'You'll have to own up, Florizella. You'll have to tell your parents. They're really worried about you.'

'Bother,' she said. 'Yes, I suppose so. Will the guards let me out if I bang on the door?'

'Try roaring!' said Bennett with a chuckle. 'No! Wait, Florizella. Check yourself out!'

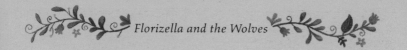

Florizella glanced in a mirror and gave a little gasp. Her hair was as wild as a lion's mane, and her face and hands were filthy from cleaning the cubs and tearing up their meat.

'A lion!' Bennett said. 'Not much risk of you turning into a lion, I'd say. You look more like a werewolf!'

'*Roar,*' said Florizella, who never cared what she looked like. She washed her face and hands, brushed her hair, then tapped on the bedroom door and called out, quite politely, 'Guard! Please tell my mother or my father that I would like to talk to them.'

Of course, the guard brought the king at once. And the queen. And the royal enchanter. And the captain of the guard. And half a dozen extra guards in case of difficulties. And the local

lion-tamer. And the deputy royal enchanter. And another enchanter who had happened to call at the palace that day, and was interested to see a princess turning into a lion.

They threw open Florizella's door, with their swords and nets and toasting forks and magic wands and stools at the ready . . . and saw Florizella, looking quite herself. They also saw Bennett – who shouldn't have been there at all – but he looked perfectly normal too. And . . . they saw four hungry little wolf cubs, who threw back their heads at all the noise and the bustle and said, 'Ki-yi-yi-yi-yi!'

CHAPTER FIVE

*Florizella finds it is hard
to say goodbye*

Florizella had hoped her parents would be pleased to discover that she was not enchanted, but had merely adopted a family of wolf cubs, but she was disappointed. For some reason they were not delighted to see her bedroom wrecked and tonight's dinner spread around the floor in chewed bits.

The queen ordered the wolf cubs to be taken to the kennels *at once*, and told Florizella

that she could keep them until they were big enough to hunt for themselves – and then they must be taken back to the forest . . . *At once!*

'I never get anything I want,' Florizella grumbled to Bennett.

It was fun keeping the wolf cubs, but they grew very fast. Within a couple of weeks they were too big for Bennett and Florizella to play with all four of them. They were too rough – they thought they were just bouncing around, but when two of them jumped up at Florizella at the same time they sent her flying into the straw bales.

A week later and Florizella and Bennett had to give up taking the cubs out for a daily walk. If they all walked in the same direction, it was

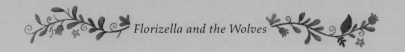

just about possible. But when they all went in different directions Bennett and Florizella were towed across the yard like a pair of mad waterskiers behind four motorboats. It was hopeless.

Worst of all, the cubs thought of themselves as a pack. Samson was pack leader. As soon as they saw any other animal – a hen in the castle yard, one of the guard's horses, or even one of the king's golden carp minding its own business in the pond – they got themselves into a pack and *stalked* it. When the king caught them stalking his fish, he was extremely cross. Not even Florizella could argue that they were helpless cubs who needed protection. They were four half-grown wolves, and they had to be free.

'Take them back to the forest,' the king said at breakfast one day. 'Go on, Florizella. It's kinder to them in the long run. Go with Bennett and leave them somewhere in the forest.'

So Florizella sent a message over to Bennett's castle by carrier pigeon. She was in a hurry so she asked the pigeon if it would mind riding a firework rocket, and very obligingly it did. It was there in a whoosh, and Bennett rode over at once. The two of them, with four big wolf cubs loping cheerfully behind, rode into the darkest, wildest part of the Purple Forest. Florizella and Bennett pulled out four large steaks from their saddlebags and put them down on the grass. The wolf cubs leaped on the food as if they were starving. They tried to steal

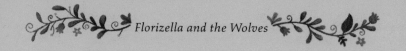

each other's share, rolling over and over and play-fighting with each other, then snatching the steaks and running off with them.

'Come on, Florizella,' Bennett said softly. 'They're all right. Let's go before they miss us.'

So Florizella and Bennett rode away as quickly as they could, leaving the wolf cubs behind.

Florizella cried all the way home, and Bennett was a bit sniffy too.

Everyone was very nice to them at the castle because they understood that it was hard to leave the wolf cubs. The queen ordered Florizella's favourite dinner: roast chicken, roast potatoes, peas and carrots, and plum

crumble for pudding. With ice cream.

The king was very sympathetic. 'Don't be sad, Florizella. I'm sure you'll see them again one day. Undoubtedly. *Undootedly!*'

Florizella saw them again sooner than she expected.

The very next day, in fact.

She had left their old kennel door open and when she went to see Jellybean the next morning, four wolf cubs came swarming out, thrilled to see her, and hungry for their breakfast after their long trot back from the forest.

The king and the queen were firm. The wolf cubs must go back to the woods. Florizella

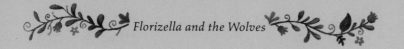

tacked up Jellybean, whistled to the cubs and led them off again, deep into the Purple Forest.

'Goodbye, little wolf cubs,' she said sadly. 'Goodbye, Samson.'

When Florizella went to bed that night, she whispered a prayer for her wolf cubs, and Samson the pack leader, and cried herself to sleep.

She didn't sleep for long.

In the middle of the night there was a great 'Ki-yi-yi-yi-yi!' from the garden. Florizella jumped awake at once and ran to look out of her bedroom window. There was the fattest, naughtiest wolf cub, Samson, sitting underneath the moon and singing for her at

the top of his squeaky little voice. When he saw
her face at the window, he stopped and grinned
with his white wolf teeth.

Florizella said, 'Oh no!' very softly. She
opened her window and climbed down the
drainpipe. Samson was *delighted* to see her
and bounced around the garden, wanting to
play.

Florizella took him firmly by his soft ear, led

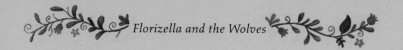

him to the kennels and shut him up for the night.

The next day she took him back to the Purple Forest again.

She didn't cry when she went to sleep that night. She was hoping he would be all right . . . but she was hoping a lot more that she'd seen the last of him.

But that night, at about midnight: 'Ki-yi-yi-yi-yi!' The next day she took him away again!

Five times Florizella took the wolf cub back to the Purple Forest. Five times he found his way home along the moonlit paths to sit under Florizella's window and howl: 'Ki-yi-yi-yi-yi!'

On the sixth day, Florizella gave up. She sent a message to the Land of the Deep Lakes for Prince Bennett to come and tell her what she could do about the wolf cub who wouldn't go home.

CHAPTER SIX

*Bennett has a plan
that turns out to
be brilliant*

When he arrived, Prince Bennett had *A Plan*.

It was a really great plan with deception and hair dye.

He took Florizella to Mrs Fitzherbert's shop, which sold useful white-magic spells and speciality teas. Bennett looked carefully along the shelves and showed Florizella a box.

It read:

> *As yellow as Goldilocks! The hair dye for all would-be golden-haired goodie-goodies!*

'What do we do with that?' Florizella asked.

'We transform him,' Bennett said mysteriously.

As soon as they got back to the palace, they caught Samson – who thought it was all a new and exciting game – and washed him thoroughly. Then they smeared the dye all over him and left it on for half an hour. When they rinsed him clean, his coat was as golden as the royal crowns. They had left the dye on his tail a little bit too long – it was slightly

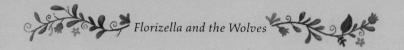

green – but they thought no one would notice. They cleaned his teeth. They brushed him well. They even put a pink bow round his neck with a label that read:

My name is Samson. I belong to Princess Florizella. Please love me.

'Ewww!' said Florizella.

Even Bennett thought that might be going a bit far. But they agreed that nothing that might help with Samson's transformation from wolf into lapdog should be left out.

When he was looking as sweet and as tame as could be, they took him to the king and told him that they'd found this golden puppy and

could Florizella possibly keep him?

The king said yes.

The king said it looked like a well-bred dog to him.

The king said it might make a very useful guard dog around the palace.

Florizella gulped down all the lies, and smiled and said, 'Thank you,' and hoped for the best.

To Florizella's surprise, Samson the wolf cub settled down very well to being a palace guard dog, and nobody ever thought that he'd had anything to do with the wolves.

He even learned to bark during the day, and though he *would* howl when there was a full moon, the king slept heavily at nights and did not hear him.

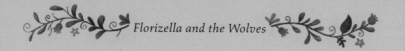

During the day, Samson would follow the king everywhere, sitting under the breakfast table, resting his chin on the king's feet, sitting at his side in the royal office. He ignored the golden carp in the pond with an air of utter disdain. He pottered with the king among the roses and made a point of eating greenfly when the king was looking. The king loved him doing that.

In the end, everyone accepted the big golden puppy as the palace dog. No one ever realised that under the dyed blond hair was a wild wolf.

Every day when Florizella went riding, Samson went too, running alongside Jellybean. Some days Florizella rode beside the river, sometimes she went to the seaside. One day she was late home and took a shortcut through

an especially wild part of a forest. She didn't see a dark shadow on a low branch of a tree. Samson didn't see it, either.

Jellybean saw it . . . but too late!

It was a black jaguar crouched low and silent, and as Florizella rode underneath the tree the jaguar crashed down on to Jellybean's plump bottom. Jellybean neighed in terror and reared up, shaking the jaguar loose and dumping Florizella on the ground. In a second the horse had raced off. The jaguar took three swift steps after him, then swung round and started coming for Florizella instead!

The jaguar's green eyes flashed like jade. Florizella turned and ran as fast as she could for the nearest tree, jumping up to catch the lowest branch. Then she swarmed upwards, climbing

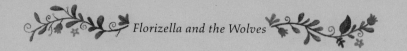

like a monkey to get away from the jaguar.

This was a good plan with one great flaw: jaguars can climb trees too. And they can climb rather better than princesses. With one smooth bound, the jaguar started up after her, its razor-sharp claws digging into the bark of the tree trunk. But just as it started up the tree, there was a great *How-how-howl!* of rage, and Samson raced towards the jaguar and leaped and bit, fastening his teeth on to its fat black tail.

That gave Florizella the chance she needed. Up and up she went until she reached the small branches where the heavy jaguar could not follow her. Then she turned and screamed to Samson to fetch help from the palace. The wolf dropped the jaguar's tail and the jaguar

turned round, snarling and slashing at him, but Samson was too quick. He streaked away in the direction of the palace, howling, 'Ki-yi-yi-yi-yi!' as he went.

Florizella gave a cheer in a rather scared voice when she saw Samson racing off. But then she fell silent. Down at the foot of the tree, the jaguar had realised that it could not climb up and get Florizella. But it did not go away. It settled down, eyed Florizella and licked its lips.

At first Florizella thought how silly it was to sit there, tail curled round its paws like a big black cat.

Then she thought how scary it was to sit there, waiting and waiting.

And *then* she realised that the jaguar was a lot smarter than she'd thought. She was

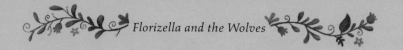

cold and tired and soon would not be able to hold tightly to the thin branch where she was clinging. And when that happened . . . she would drop out of the tree like a sweet little plum . . . straight into the open smiling jaws of the black jaguar.

Florizella's cold fingers tightened on the branch. She knew she would not be able to hold on forever.

It all depended on Samson.

CHAPTER SEVEN

*Samson wins
his place*

ack at the royal palace no one took any notice of Samson when he came racing over the drawbridge. He howled and howled and whined, and people just called to him to be quiet. One of the royal guards checked that his water bowl was filled and then tried to catch him to shut him in the kennels.

Samson ducked away and raced into the

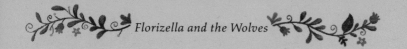

royal office where the queen was eating bread and honey. She really hated bread and honey, but it's in the Queen's Rules. Samson charged right up to her and barked.

'Mmmdown! Mmood dog,' the queen said through a sticky mouthful.

Samson turned round and ran up to the king. He hurled himself into his lap and put his fat paddy paws on his shoulders and howled straight into his face.

'It's Florizella!' said the king at once. 'The dog's speaking to me. He's telling me something must have happened to Florizella! *Undootedly!*'

Just at that moment a groom came running from the stable. 'Princess Florizella's pony has come home without her!' he announced.

'Again,' he said, which was a bit unnecessary.

'Mmmummon the guard!' the queen started up.

'Undootedly! Summon the guard!' the king repeated more clearly.

At once the royal guards came scrambling out of the guardroom and leaped on their horses. Samson dashed ahead of them along the twisty path through the woods, and they blew *Tooroo! Tooroo!* on their horns as they galloped.

Florizella heard the sound of them coming and tightened her grip on the branch for a few moments more. The jaguar heard them too and leaped up towards Florizella's dangling feet. For one dreadful moment, Florizella thought she could not pull her feet out of reach of those big black paws. Then the jaguar growled angrily at her, turned away and slunk off into the darkness.

The guards halted and jumped off. They gathered round the tree, calling up to ask Florizella if she was all right. She said, 'Yes,' but then found she had frozen with fright. She couldn't move.

The topmost branches of the tree were too thin to hold anyone but a light girl like

Florizella, so no one could climb up to her –
and now she was too cold and scared to climb
down. The captain of the guard swung her own
scarlet cape off her shoulders and spread it out.
The guards took the four corners and stretched
it tight.

'Jump, Florizella!' said the captain in her
clear voice. No one *ever* disobeyed her.

Florizella, colder and more scared than
she'd ever been in her life before, shut her eyes
tight and dropped out of the tree like a baby
owl tumbling from a nest . . .

. . . *BOING!* into the cape.

Samson was the hero of the day, for fighting
the jaguar and for running to get help. But

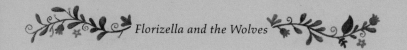

everyone had noticed that he had not barked once. He had howled . . . and his howl was a wolf's howl.

Bennett and Florizella took Samson to see the king and queen and told the truth at last: that Samson the wonder-dog was really a wolf. Indeed, he was one of the wolf cubs who should have gone back to the forest. Bennett owned up that it was his plan to disguise Samson as a golden dog, and Florizella told them how much she loved Samson and wanted to keep him.

The king and queen were too pleased with him and too grateful to think of sending him back to the forest.

'I think he's earned his place here,' the queen said.

'He can stay,' agreed the king. It was a sunny day and he wanted to be out in his garden. 'But there are conditions,' he added as he went to the door. 'All visitors to the palace must be told that he is a dog. I won't have it said we keep a wolf in the palace – people would think it odd. And if his brothers or sisters turn up they must go back to the forest. I won't live with an actual pack of wolves. This is a palace. It's not suitable.'

Bennett and Florizella nodded hard. They looked like very obedient children.

'*And* another thing,' said the king grumpily. 'He's to eat ordinary meat – not my venison.'

Bennett and Florizella nodded again and tried to look angelic.

'And if he grows up and has wolf cubs of his own—'

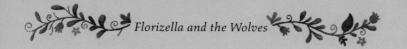

'Oh! *Newborn wolf cubs!*' Florizella interrupted in delight, forgetting to look obedient.

Bennett kicked her gently on the ankle to warn her to be quiet.

'They are *not* to be brought here,' the king said firmly.

Florizella looked as if she might argue.

Bennett leaned against her shoulder in a silencing sort of way. 'We'll think of something,' he said very quietly.

'I do keep wishing that this could be an ordinary sort of a palace,' the king said to himself as he went out into his garden. 'Just an ordinary sort of kingdom, for an ordinary sort of king, with everyone following the Rules. Just for once.'

Samson nodded very seriously as if he had thought this over and wished it could be an ordinary sort of palace too, then trotted out into the rose garden after the king.

Bennett and Florizella went over to the window and saw the king pottering among the roses, with Samson following behind him, licking greenflies off the rosebuds whenever the king looked his way.

'Good boy,' said the king softly, so that no one would hear.

'Ki-yi-yi-yi-yi!' said Samson.

Florizella and the Giant

CHAPTER ONE

One huge problem and a mammoth picnic

What terror there is in the Seven Kingdoms!

A giant has arrived. A giant bigger than any giant that anyone has ever seen before.

A super-giant.

A mega-giant.

An absolutely *giant* giant for which there is only one suitable word:

Mountainous.

So say the people of the Plain Green Plains in the south of the Seven Kingdoms – and they should know because it is their flat, plain green fields that the giant tramples every day, and their crops that are squashed every time he sits down to take a nap, and their houses that are shaken to pieces every time he does a little jog or a little jig or a little wriggle, or whatever it is that he is doing up there.

For no one can see what it is that he is doing up there.

No one can see whether he is red-faced and running, or smiling and dancing, or yawning and stretching. All that anyone has ever seen of him are his huge (super-huge) trampling (trampling everything) boots. No one has even seen his head – it is too high up.

'Hidden by clouds,' the messenger says.

'Well, I don't believe one word of it,' Princess Florizella said to her particular friend, Prince Bennett. They were sitting behind her parents' thrones, listening to the messenger from the Plain Green Plains gasping for breath and shaking with fright as he told the king and the queen of the Seven Kingdoms about the giant, and the people of the Plain Green Plains and the footprints that are as big as lakes.

'*Something must be done!*' the messenger finished.

'Like what?' Florizella muttered to Bennett.

'*At once!*' the messenger started up again.

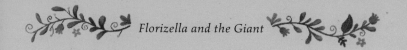

'By who?' Bennett whispered back.

The king looked very worried. 'When was the last time we had a giant?' he asked the court herald.

She consulted the scroll. 'Ages ago, Your Majesty,' she said. 'In your father's father's father's father's time. The king (your father's father's father's father) went out and challenged the giant to single combat and slew him after three days of bloody battle, in which he was nearly killed three times over!'

'Well, we don't want any of that, I'm sure,' the king said hastily. 'Why don't we just ask him to move on?'

There was a muffled giggle from Bennett, still hidden by the big gold throne. 'Not into my kingdom, thank you very much,' he said

to Florizella. 'We don't want a giant any more than you do!'

The messenger from the Plain Green Plains shook his head. 'We have tried asking the giant to move,' he said. 'He responds to nothing. We have shouted at him and written letters to him. We sent him a petition. We had a demonstration. We had a protest march and a pop festival. He just keeps trampling on our crops and scooping up whole barnfuls of wheat and taking them off. He gathers forests of saplings like a child might pick daisies. He scoops up fish ponds in his hand and drinks them dry. Your Majesty *must* save us!'

'Yes,' said the king thoughtfully. 'I can see you might think it should be me.' He turned to the queen. 'Any ideas, my love?' he asked.

'Anyone you think might be more suitable as a challenger? Than, for example . . . ME?'

The queen nodded briskly. 'Send the royal surveyor,' she said. 'He's good at measuring things. He's just come back from mapping the Red Mountains. He can measure the giant for us and estimate how we can move him, and where he should be placed. We need to know a lot more about him before we take any action.'

'And send the royal zookeeper too,' the king said. 'She might have some idea about capturing him and feeding him.'

'And an enchanter to be on the safe side,' the queen said. 'I'd never trust a surveyor without an enchanter to keep an eye on him.'

'An expedition!' the king said cheerfully. 'We'll *all* go.'

The messenger from the Plain Green Plains dropped to his knees. 'I thank Your Majesties!' he said. 'I'll ride straight home and tell my people you are coming at once to save them. We will expect you immediately.'

'At once!' the king said. 'Undoubtedly!' He stood up and waved his sceptre with a flourish. '*Undootedly!*'

'At once!' everybody said, waving back at him happily. '*Undootedly!*'

'It'll take four days at least, for this lot to get packed, never mind started!' said Florizella to Bennett, still hidden behind the thrones. 'We'd better get our ponies and leave now, and see this giant before everyone else arrives and ruins it.'

Bennett nodded and the two of them slid

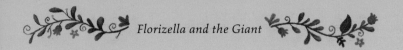

very carefully through the curtains at the back of the thrones, through the hidden door and then across the hall to the castle kitchens. 'I'll saddle up the ponies; you get a picnic,' said Bennett. 'See you at the front gateway in five minutes.'

Into two rucksacks Florizella piled the following:

Boiled eggs (4)
Slices of ham (8)
Bread rolls (6)
Lettuce and watercress
Tomatoes
Corn on the cob (4)

Meat pies (2)

Sausage rolls (10)

Cheese

Crisps

Those crispy things that look like seashells and are crunchy when you put them in your mouth but then go all deliciously squashy and you have to eat another one. No one in the entire history of the universe has ever eaten only one – unless it was a test. (3 packets)

Peanuts

Salted biscuits

Lemonade (4 bottles)

Bars of chocolate (12)

Chocolate biscuits

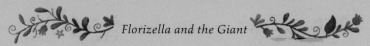

Chocolate cake

Chocolate pudding

(Florizella was rather fond of chocolate.)

Popcorn (4 large bags)

Peaches (8)

Strawberries (4 punnets)

Raspberries (8 punnets)

Gooseberries (2 punnets)

Plums

Greengages

Apricots

Apples

(Florizella was rather fond of fruit too.)

They were rather large and bulky rucksacks once all that was crammed inside, but Florizella thought that you can never take too much

food on a serious adventure. You never know how long you will be away from home, and if matters get desperate you can always use it for ammunition.

She dashed upstairs and fetched her best sword from her bedroom, and then ran out of the castle, lugging the rucksacks, to meet Bennett at the gate. As she ran she whistled for Samson, the disguised wolf cub, who came lolloping out of the stableyard, his coat very golden in the sunshine, the ribbon round his neck very pink.

The portcullis was up; the drawbridge was down. No one stopped the prince and princess and asked them where they were going and if they were allowed. Everyone was used to the two of them riding all over the place on

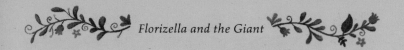

their own. The gate guard said, 'Halt!' as they clattered out of the yard . . . and finished, 'Who goes there?' as they disappeared down the road. Then he said, 'I s'pose that's OK, then,' and went back inside the guardhouse where he'd been reading an extremely interesting fairy story to the other guards.

Very soon, Bennett and Florizella, mounted on their fine ponies with Samson loping behind them, were trotting briskly down the white chalky road that wound far ahead, round the hills and woods, over hill and valley and indeed stream, southwards to the Plain Green Plains.

CHAPTER TWO

*Bennett has a genius
plan that does not
fully succeed*

It is rather an extraordinary experience, hunting a giant. You don't need dogs to smell him out, as you would if you were hunting pheasant or duck. The smell of a giant, even an extremely clean giant, wafts all around him for about ten kilometres in any direction. This particular giant had found a store of onions on the very morning that Florizella and Bennett arrived at the Plain

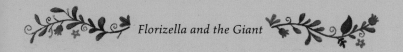

Green Plains, and the smell of his breath was enough to knock them off horseback.

'Yuck,' said Florizella, clinging to the mane of her brilliant bay pony, Jellybean, while warm gales of onion-scented wind buffeted them.

Samson let out a short, yappy howl. 'Ki-yi-yi-yi-yi!' His nose was burning with too much scent and his eyes were watering.

When hunting a giant, you don't need sharp eyesight to spot him. He's not like deer that can disappear into a forest, or sleek hares that lie low and blend into the ground – this giant blocked the sunlight. His feet and legs, thicker and bigger than tree trunks, towered above the flat, fertile lands of the Plain Green Plains.

Jellybean stopped dead a good kilometre

from the giant boots. So did Bennett's pony, Thunderer, and they both kept a close watch on a giant bootlace as big as a rope from a sailing ship, which was undone and snaking across the road.

Samson blinked miserably and growled under his breath.

This really was a very big giant indeed. Florizella and Bennett had been privately certain that the messenger from the Plain Green Plains had been exaggerating about the size of the giant. Their high spirits on the day-long ride had been because they thought they were on their way to a giant perhaps three metres tall. But now they were close to him they could see why the messenger had been so determined that the king himself

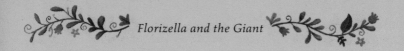

should come and sort out the problem. The adventure suddenly seemed *very* serious.

Even sitting on their horses, Bennett and Florizella were only just level with the giant's ankles in his thick knitted socks. Standing on the ground, they only came up to his big polished toecaps. They couldn't even see his head. His broad legs, dressed in socks and big baggy breeches, and his tummy, straining against a green jerkin and belt, blocked the view upwards like an overhanging balcony on a house.

Florizella and Bennett got off their horses and turned them loose in a nearby field. The horses kicked up their heels, rushed over to the far side and tried, very foolishly, to hide behind a tree. Horses *hate* giants and

Jellybean especially disliked Florizella's more dangerous adventures.

'I have a plan,' said Bennett. 'We will summon him to a parley. And then we will issue our challenge to him.'

'Challenging him to what?' Florizella asked.

'Single combat with sword and lance,' Bennett said promptly. 'You'll have to fight him, Florizella. It's your kingdom, after all.'

'Not me,' Florizella said equally promptly. 'You must be crazy, Bennett. It would be like a mouse challenging one of us to single combat. I think we should talk to him. He may be lost. Or just passing through.'

'Combat would be more princely,' Bennett said regretfully. 'But I suppose you're right. How shall we talk to him?'

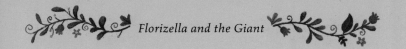

'We need a white flag,' Florizella said. 'To show that we want a peaceful talk. Have you got a clean hankie?'

Bennett just laughed. Neither of them *ever* had a clean handkerchief.

'We'll use your shirt,' Florizella said. 'It's white under the dirt. And, anyway, we're not asking him to check up on the laundry. We just want to attract his attention and show him we mean peace.'

Bennett took off his shirt and they tied it to a fallen branch of a tree. Then they went as close to the giant boots as they thought safe and waved the flag in the air.

They waved for a long time.

Nothing happened.

'I don't think he can see us,' Florizella said.

'My arms are tired,' Bennett said. 'Let's shout at him.'

The two children bawled upwards. 'EXCUSE US! WE WANT TO TALK TO YOU!'

Absolutely nothing happened.

'This is stupid,' Florizella said. 'We'll have to get him to look down. I'll stab him in the ankle with my sword.'

'Better not,' Bennett said cautiously. 'It might hurt him.'

'No,' Florizella said. 'Look at the thickness of his socks. It would only be like a little mosquito bite.'

'Mm,' said Bennett. 'And what do people do to mosquitoes?'

'Swat them,' Florizella replied. Then she said, 'Oh, I see.'

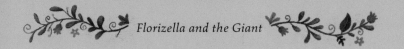

'We have to get him down to our level, without making him angry,' Bennett said thoughtfully. He was staring at the great rope of bootlace. Then he snapped his fingers. 'I am a genius!' he said. 'We'll knot his bootlace to that tree, then he'll notice it has come undone and kneel down to do it up. Then he'll see us, and we can talk to him.'

'Great,' said Florizella.

The two of them took hold of the rope and, with much heaving and shoving, got it tied round a sturdy oak that grew in a little copse of other trees at the side of the road.

Samson sat down beside the rope and tried to look optimistic. He was a *very* unhappy wolf cub.

'Look out!' Florizella yelled. 'He's moving!'

She was right.

One giant boot strode forward. The other one that was securely fastened to the oak tree moved a little. The rope strained tight, tight, tighter, and then . . .

. . . *pee-yoing!*

The rope snapped, the great boot shot forward, the giant stumbled and with a crash like a thousand earthquakes he fell to the earth, crushing two fences and sprawling over four fields.

'Well done, genius!' Florizella said crossly. 'Now he's knocked himself out!'

The two children walked past the fallen body to the giant's head. It was as big as a small hill. His skin was as rugged and as rough as a pebbly beach. His beard was a forest of thick golden hair. The hair on his head was a jungle of curls. He had fallen with his head turned to one side, and he was smiling slightly as if he were having pleasant dreams.

'What shall we do now?' Florizella asked

Bennett. 'Have you got another plan?'

'Wait till he wakes up, I suppose,' Bennett said. 'I hope he won't have a headache,' he added a little nervously. 'I think he hit his head as he fell.'

'He can't eat us,' Florizella said without thinking. Then she said, 'Oh! I suppose he *could*.'

A small crowd of people of the Plain Green Plains had come running when they'd heard the great thunder of the falling giant.

'Cut his throat, Princess Florizella!' someone shouted from the back of the crowd. 'Before he wakes up.'

'Certainly not!' Florizella and Bennett both said at once.

'He's eaten all our food and destroyed hundreds

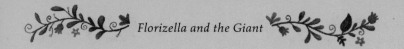

of houses,' a woman cried. 'He should be punished.'

'In the old days a true prince would have challenged him to single combat,' a man said, looking at Bennett.

'Those days are gone,' Bennett said firmly. 'Anyway, we don't want to kill him – we just want to move him on somewhere else.'

The giant stirred slightly. Everyone in the crowd – especially the people who had talked very boldly about cutting his throat, or challenging him to single combat – rushed backwards and stayed out of reach. Only Florizella and Bennett waited where they were, right in front of the giant's face.

Slowly the giant opened his huge blue eyes.

'Hello,' Florizella squeaked. Because she

was scared, her voice came out too high. She tried again. 'Hello!' she said, trying for a deep, comforting voice. This time she sounded like a cow mooing.

'This is the land of the Seven Kingdoms,' Bennett bellowed. 'This is Her Royal Highness, Florizella, princess of this realm. I am Prince Bennett of the next-door kingdom, the Land of Deep Lakes.' He bowed very politely, then he glanced back at Florizella. 'She really *is* a princess,' he added. 'She looks like a princess when she is clean.'

Florizella scowled at Bennett. 'I welcome you to my country,' she said politely to the giant. 'Er . . . will you be staying long?'

The giant's blue eyes at once filled with great round pools of tears.

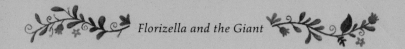

'*Unh-hunh*,' he bellowed.

He was crying with great loud sobs, so noisy that they were like thunderclaps roaring one after another. Florizella and Bennett were bowled over by the blast of his grief. They clung to each other on the ground while the onion-scented gale nearly blew them away.

Samson tried to rush to Florizella's side, but was blown over and over until he got stuck in a bush.

'Go up!' Bennett yelled in Florizella's ear. '*Up!* Away from his mouth!'

The two of them, clinging to bushes and grass, crawled away from the giant's mouth towards his nose.

'*Unh-hunh! Unh-hunh! Unh-hunh!*'

The giant was sobbing now as if he would

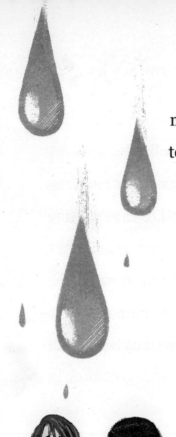

never stop. Great fat, round tears as big as boulders rained down on Florizella and Bennett, drenching them with warm, salty water as they struggled to get away from the hurricane of the giant's sorrow.

'Stop crying!' Florizella yelled. '*Stop crying!*'

'*Unh-hunh!*' the giant went, as loudly as ever.

'*What's the matter?*' Bennett shouted.

A huge teardrop splashed to the ground, drenching them both as if someone

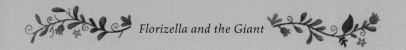

was throwing buckets of warm water at them.

'I'm hungry! And I'm l-l-*lost*!'

Another thunderstorm of tears poured down upon the children. Another ear-splitting sob nearly blew them away.

'We can't survive much more of this!' Bennett yelled to Florizella. 'He must stop!'

Florizella nodded. 'Shove me up towards his ear,' she said.

Bennett bent down and pushed Florizella up towards the giant's bushy yellow beard, and then higher – to the great dark cavern of his earhole.

'Don't fall in!' Bennett yelled. 'Don't go near the edge.'

Florizella nodded and took a firm grip on the soft undergrowth of the giant's beard. 'We

are your friends!' she bawled down the cave of his earhole. 'We will get you some food. We will help you find your way home. STOP CRYING!'

The giant stopped suddenly. The silence was so startling after the roaring sobs and crashing tears that Bennett shook his head, thinking he had gone deaf.

Samson struggled out of the bushes and sat down sulkily to lick his paws.

'You'll be my friend?' the giant said. The earth shook slightly. Behind Bennett a tree crashed to the ground.

'You must whisper!' Florizella shouted. 'You nearly blew us away just now. We are very small. You have to whisper to us.'

'You'll be my friend?' the giant whispered.

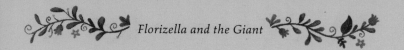

Cautiously, Bennett sat up. 'Yes!' he yelled. 'And we will help you. What are you doing in this country?'

The giant's huge lower lip quivered. His eyes filled with tears.

'He's off again!' Bennett yelled to Florizella. 'Watch out!'

'DON'T CRY!' Florizella shouted. 'We will help you! There's nothing to cry about!'

'There isn't?' the giant asked hopefully.

'NO! Not at all!' the two children yelled together.

A little smile came across the giant's huge, handsome, moon face. 'I was hungry,' he said. 'I don't have a mother or a father to care for me. I'm an orphan. I live alone and I have to

grow my own food.' His lower lip trembled.

'Watch out,' Bennett said warningly, getting a good grip round a small tree trunk.

'But I can't read the writing on the seed packets that I bought to plant in my garden. I thought I had planted tomato seeds and lettuce seeds, but all that came up were flowers.'

Florizella dropped down from the giant's beard and stood beside Bennett.

'Poppies!' the giant said sadly. 'Very pretty. But I was hungry.'

'You poor thing,' Florizella said comfortingly.

The giant's huge misty blue eyes turned towards her. He let out a soft sob.

'Don't be nice to him,' Bennett said urgently. 'You'll set him off again.'

'You're very kind.' The giant snuffled a little.

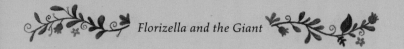

'Like a friend. I've never had a proper friend.'

'Watch out,' Bennett said. 'Here we go.'

'Don't cry!' Florizella yelled. 'I would never be friends with a crybaby.'

With a great gulp, the giant swallowed his sorrow. 'I'll try not to,' he said humbly. 'But I've come an awfully long way, and I've been very lonely and very hungry. I left my little cottage weeks ago. I walked and walked until I came here. There were lots of things to eat when I arrived. But there seems to be less now.'

'That's because you've eaten it all!' Bennett shouted severely. 'Perhaps you should go on.'

The giant sat up. The little wood shook as he moved. He put his hand down and the two children climbed into the warm palm. He lifted them up in the air, higher, higher, higher, until

they were level with his face and he could see them. He sighed sadly. Bennett and Florizella clung to his thumb until the storm passed.

'But I'm lost,' he said sorrowfully. 'I can't find my way home now. It's horrible being lost, and hungry, and not knowing your way home.'

Florizella and Bennett glanced at each other. 'We know the direction you came from,' Bennett said. 'We could put you on the right road. Would you know your way from the borders of the Seven Kingdoms?' He paused. 'Avoiding the Land of Deep Lakes?' he suggested. Bennett didn't think his mother and father, the king and queen of the Land of Deep Lakes, would be too pleased if he directed a huge and hungry giant across their realm.

The giant shook his enormous head. 'I

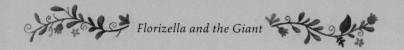

don't think so. I couldn't see very well. I just wandered around, but it was all a blur to me. And what shall I do when I get home? There'll be nothing for me to eat. I've got nothing to plant in my garden, and I need the right seeds. Vegetable seeds.'

'But, if we gave you some vegetable seeds from our gardeners, they would grow too small, wouldn't they?' Florizella asked.

'Not in my country,' the giant said a little more cheerfully. 'It's just great there. As soon as anything is planted into the earth of my country it grows to the right size for us. Our tomatoes grow as big as your elephants!' He snuffled. 'But I can't even see your elephants clearly!'

'Don't worry about that,' Bennett reassured him. 'We didn't bring any elephants with us.'

The giant bent down to peer at the horses. The horses, insulted, looked right back at him.

'Sorry,' he said.

Florizella tugged at Bennett's arm. 'D'you think his eyesight is all right?' she whispered. 'He couldn't read the seed packets, and he couldn't see where he was going. If he can't even see elephants, he must be very short-sighted!'

'A short-sighted giant would have *real* trouble,' Bennett said. 'He'd have to be long-sighted just to be able to see his feet.'

'Have you ever been able to see things clearly?' Florizella yelled at the giant.

Slowly he shook his big handsome head. 'No. I couldn't see the blackboard at school, or my books. Everybody just thought I was stupid.'

His big mouth turned down again. 'Stupid,' he said sadly. 'They called me stupid at school.'

'We don't think you're stupid,' Bennett said quickly. 'We like you. We said that we will be your friends. What's your name?'

'Simon,' the giant said solemnly. 'My name is Simon. I'm very pleased to meet you.'

Bennett did his most princely bow. 'I'm pleased to meet you too, Simon,' he said kindly. 'And we're going to help you. Wait right there and we'll be back in a little while.'

'All right,' Simon the giant said.

'You have to put us down,' Florizella pointed out.

'Oh yes,' he said, lowering his mighty hand to earth so that the children could jump off.

'Don't go away, Simon!' Florizella warned

him. 'Actually, don't move. We won't be long. And you don't want to tread on us!'

'Oh, I wouldn't do that! I'll stay still! I love little tiddly mice.'

'*Mice?*' Florizella asked Bennett. 'Did he say mice?'

'Never mind that now,' Bennett said quickly. 'We've got an awful lot to do. We've got to feed him and get him something to drink. We've got to persuade everyone not to challenge him to combat.'

'That won't be too hard!' Florizella said, nodding towards the people of the Plain Green Plains, who were still keeping a very safe distance away.

'And we've got to solve all his problems!' Bennett went on.

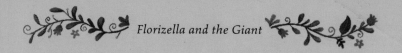

Florizella stopped dead. '*All of them!* How?' she asked.

'Glasses!' Bennett said triumphantly. 'We're going to make him a pair of glasses!'

CHAPTER FOUR

*Florizella and Bennett
make the biggest picnic
the world has ever seen*

Within an hour, Bennett had the Seven Kingdoms' fire brigade – all twenty-three fire engines – lined up beside the largest lake in the kingdom, pumping kilos of sugar and litres of lemon juice into it, and then pumping the whole sticky, sweet, glorious lake of lemonade into their enormous tanks.

All the children from the nearest school – Great Valley Lake School – played truant for

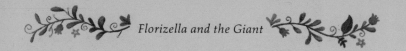

the whole day and went down to the lakeside with straws and sucked until they were blue in the face from lack of air, and then green in the face from too much lemonade.

Then, with Bennett sitting beside the driver on the box of the leading fire engine (he had always longed to do that) *and* with the siren going *Honk! Honk! Honk!*, the entire brigade of twenty-three fire engines went roaring down the road to the Plain Green Plains where the giant was sitting patiently, as still as a rock in the little wood, waiting for Florizella and Bennett to come back.

The firemen unpacked their thickest and longest hosepipe and held it up to the giant. Simon put it carefully into his cavernous mouth, and then they pumped a steady stream

of sweet lemonade up to him, emptying every one of the twenty-three fire engines until at last the giant burped an earth-shattering burp and said, 'Pardon me.'

Meanwhile Florizella, mounted on Jellybean with Samson trotting behind her – very fast away from the giant, rather slowly back towards him – was riding round to every nearby farmhouse asking everyone to come at once and to bring all the food they had in their larder for the biggest picnic in history.

They weren't at all keen. There were still a number of people who thought the giant should be murdered while he slept. There were even more who thought the king and queen – or Florizella and Bennett – should move him on without delay. But Florizella, who could be

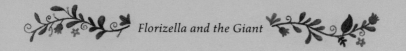

very persuasive, told them all that the only way they would get rid of the giant for good would be to feed him up, equip him with glasses and seeds, then help him to go home.

'He doesn't want to stay!' she said. 'So we have to help him find his way home. Besides, he doesn't mean any harm. He's only little.'

How Florizella could call an enormous giant 'little' was beyond most people. But the nicer people felt sorry for Simon. And the crosser ones were not going to attack him on their own. So Florizella got her way and very soon led them all, in wagons and farm carts, coaches and carriages, to the wood on the Plain Green Plains where the giant was obediently sitting as still as he could.

They built great bonfires. They roasted oxen

on spits as big as trees. They piled mound upon mound of bread dough into bathtubs and set them to cook on the hot embers. They baked a thousand potatoes in the hot ashes, they trailed string after string of sausages like bunting through the flames, where they cooked and spat and sizzled. They found a big empty swimming pool from somewhere and threw hundreds of lettuces into it, tomatoes by the thousand and lorry-loads of onions for a fresh salad.

'Not *more* onions!' Florizella said.

They went to a garden centre and bought the biggest ornamental fishpond that anyone had ever seen, with a lovely circular wavy edge, and into it they poured all the milk from the dairy and all the custard powder they could lay their

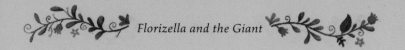

hands on. They stirred it up and then poured a long stream of red jelly on top. When it had set, which took several hours, they called out the Seven Kingdoms' world-famous weight-lifting team.

Dressed only in their smart blue trunks, their great muscles bulging with the strain, the twenty strong men stood on one side of the enormous jelly mould. At the count of three they tipped it up, slowly, slowly, slowly, until it was on its side and then crashed down on to a sheet of corrugated iron that was to be the giant's pudding plate.

They stepped back, bowed at the crowd and slapped each other on the back.

That was the first stage completed.

The second stage was even harder. They all

stood round the upside-down jelly mould and gripped the rim. They heaved and heaved and heaved, while their muscles bulged and their eyes popped out and their faces went most dreadfully red. There was an exciting moment when nothing happened, and then with a great

Flubb

  ubb

   ubb

    ubb

     ubb . . .

. . . the biggest jelly-and-custard trifle in the world slithered out of the jelly mould and sat wobbling temptingly in the sunlight like a red-and-yellow island.

When it was all ready, two hundred sea scouts from the Seven Kingdoms' navy struggled up

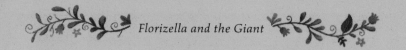

with a great sail from a tall-masted ship. Carefully they spread it out, heaved it up on to the giant's knees and heaped all the food on it.

Then the giant, using his huge fat fingers, very carefully picked up all the potatoes, sausages, bread, roasted oxen and salad, and ate and ate and ate. He used a scoop from a bulldozer to eat the trifle. It was like a dainty little teaspoon in his hand. He dug into the jelly-and-custard island, shovel after shovel, until finally it was all gone. Every delicious slurpy bit.

It was *unbelievable* how much he ate. Florizella and Bennett watched in amazement as all the food they had gathered from the length and breadth of the kingdom disappeared. Samson kept a keen lookout for any leftovers. He was determined to lick the bowl. He would

have to climb into it, of course, and wade through jelly. He was really starting to like the giant.

'Have you had enough?' Florizella yelled up at the giant. She was perching on one of his knees, clinging to his sail-napkin.

The giant beamed down at her. 'That was grand! But tell me – what's for tea?'

'We'll think about tea later,' Florizella said firmly. 'I want you to wait here now while we see if we can help you with your eyesight.'

'I've got to sit still again?' Simon asked. He was disappointed.

'Yes!' Florizella shouted at him.

'I thought friends played games together. I thought the three of *us* might play a game.'

'I have to find my mother and father,'

Florizella said quickly. 'They will want to meet you.'

'Can't we have a quick game before you go? What about Hide and Seek?'

Florizella gazed up at the enormous giant. Even sitting down, his head poked high above the tops of the smaller trees. Standing up, he was taller than the wood. The only place he would ever be able to hide would be among the highest of mountains. And then his boots would fill a small valley.

'We'll play something later,' Florizella promised. 'Will you sit still now?'

Simon was reluctant. 'Isn't there anyone who will play with me? Or even talk to me? I'd like someone to tell me a story.'

Florizella looked around. Everyone who

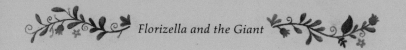

had been standing about doing nothing except listening to Florizella talking to the giant, suddenly became tremendously busy and had no time at all.

Everyone except one little girl.

She came up to Florizella and smiled a wide, gap-toothed smile. She nodded her curly head. 'I'll talk to him,' she said to Florizella. 'I think he'th thweet.'

Florizella looked doubtfully at her. She was such a small girl, dressed in a blue pinafore dress with very clean white socks and blue shoes with little straps.

'How old are you?' Florizella asked.

'Thix,' the little girl said. 'I could tell him *thtorieth*.'

Bennett gave a giggle and turned it into a

cough. The little girl was not fooled. She looked at him severely.

'There ith no need to thnigger,' she said warningly. 'I know thome very nithe thtorieth.'

Florizella grinned. 'What's your name?' she asked.

'Thethilia,' the little girl said. 'That'th unfortunate at the moment, becauthe I have a lithp while my front tooth ith growing.'

'Oh! So you have!' Florizella said kindly, pretending that she had not noticed, and scowling at Bennett, who stuffed his fist into his mouth to muffle his laughter and ducked behind some trees.

Florizella called up to the giant. 'There's a little

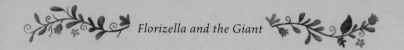

girl down here called Cecilia. She says she'll tell you stories.'

The giant lowered his great hand and Cecilia clambered into his warm, damp palm. Florizella watched as the giant raised her up to his eye level.

'Now,' she heard her say. 'I'll tell you all about *Thleeping Beauty*.'

CHAPTER FIVE

A little confusion because another word for glasses is 'spectacles' - and the word 'spectacle' also means a fabulous sort of show

The king and queen had taken a long time to get everyone in the royal court moving, but they were only an hour's journey away from the giant when Florizella and Bennett met them on the road. With the royal procession was the royal zoo keeper, the royal surveyor, the royal enchanter, two hundred of the royal guard and about a hundred other people who had nothing better to do on a fine

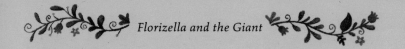

summer's day than to come along and see what was happening.

'Hello, Florizella!' the king said as Florizella came cantering up on Jellybean. 'Found the giant?'

'Yes!' Florizella said in a rush. 'He's only young and he's short-sighted and lonely. But he *will* go back to his own country if we can help him to plant his vegetable garden.'

The king blinked a bit. 'Oh, good,' he said. He smiled at the queen. 'Looks like Florizella has it under control. Perhaps we should go home and leave it all to her.'

The queen smiled. 'I'll just see this giant before we go,' she said. 'Sometimes Florizella's ideas get a little out of hand—'

'How do you make glasses?' Florizella

interrupted. 'For short sight. I need spectacles.'

'I expect I could magic a little something,' the royal enchanter offered grandly.

'Go on, then,' Florizella said.

There was a small clap of thunder, a puff of green smoke and then there, in the road before them, stood the most amazing scene. There were dancing girls with ostrich feathers in their hair, there were elephants, there were fireworks exploding brightly in the sky, there were trapeze artists, there was a railway train painted in gold with a song-and-dance ragtime band on silver wagons behind it. There were dancing bears and acrobats. There were jugglers, and fountains pouring into silver basins. There were rose petals tumbling down in scented showers from out of thin air.

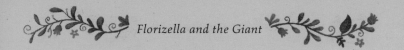

'*No, no, no!*' Florizella said crossly. 'I meant *a pair of spectacles.*'

The royal enchanter waved his wand again. There was another small explosion, and at once there was a huge Ferris wheel with dancing girls waving and singing from the swinging chairs, a showboat paddling its way up the chalky road with people tap-dancing on the top deck, and a flying circus high in the sky with beautiful girls and handsome men standing on the wings of little biplanes that trailed coloured smoke and flags. There was a brass band, a troupe of clowns, a magician pulling doves out of every pocket, which flew around in circling flocks, and about a hundred milk-white horses cantering round a circus ring.

'*No! No!*' Florizella said. 'A pair of spectacles

to help someone who is short-sighted. *Glasses!*'

'Oh, sorry,' the royal enchanter said. With a puff of blue smoke the whole thing disappeared as suddenly as it had come.

'I say, Florizella, that looked rather fun,' the king said wistfully.

'But I need glasses for the giant,' Florizella said. 'He is most dreadfully short-sighted, and until he can see properly he can't go back to his own land and plant his own garden. Is it possible to make glasses big enough to fit him?' she asked.

'I don't see why not,' the royal surveyor offered. 'It's just a question of making ordinary glasses, only ten times bigger.'

'Can we do it?' Bennett asked.

The royal surveyor took a gold pencil from

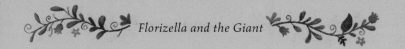

behind his ear and a piece of paper from his pocket and started doing sums for a long time, whistling softly to himself while he worked.

'If everyone in the Seven Kingdoms donated a window from every household, we would have enough glass,' he said after a long while.

He held up his hand for silence and did his sums again. 'If everyone donated a bit of their garden gates, we would have enough metal for the frames,' he said.

He did some more sums.

'If we emptied one of the small pools at the edge of Great Valley Lake, then filled it with all the windowpanes, then made an enormous bonfire with all the wood from Bear Forest on top, keeping it stoked up all the time . . . we could melt the glass into the right sort of shape

for lenses for spectacles.'

The king and queen gaped. 'Burn the wood from Bear Forest?' they asked. 'Empty the pools at the edge of Great Valley Lake?'

'Great Valley Lake is empty already,' Bennett said apologetically. 'We made it into lemonade and he drank it. Sorry.'

'This *is* an emergency,' Florizella said. 'If he can't see to plant his seeds, he can't look after himself, which means he can't go home. And everyone called him stupid at school, which isn't fair. And he *is* awfully nice.'

'Oh, all right,' the king said. 'Send out a royal proclamation . . . but people aren't going to like it.'

CHAPTER SIX

In which Cecilia proves to be one smart little girl

I n fact, the people did not mind so very much.

It is a rule in the Seven Kingdoms that anything you do not need is collected and shared. Empty bottles are washed and reused. Cardboard and paper is collected, mashed up and made into new paper. Even potato peelings, bits of vegetables and food are collected and fed to the herds of pigs,

cows and horses. If someone has a bicycle they don't use, they just paint it yellow and leave it outside their door. When someone else wants a ride, they take it and then leave it outside *their* door. When someone has a baby and it grows out of the pram, they give it to someone who has a new baby.

Once people got the idea that there were plenty of bicycles, and prams, and toys around, they forgot all about keeping them for their own. And everybody shared their food and sometimes cooked in a neighbourhood kitchen.

So the idea that since the whole kingdom had a problem with the giant, the whole kingdom had to do something about it, was not a great shock. Everyone saw at once that

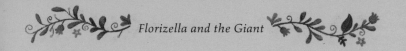

one window each was a small price to pay to help the giant. And, anyway, the summer was very fine with no rain, so they did not miss their windows as much as they would have done had it been winter.

Everyone who had fancy iron gates cut the knobs and twiddly bits off the top and brought them to a great heap of scrap iron beside the royal camp on the Plain Green Plains. They were sorry for the short-sighted giant. But more than anything else they all hoped that the plan to make him spectacles would work so that he could go home and grow his own crops, instead of eating so much of the food belonging to the Land of the Seven Kingdoms.

The royal surveyor had surveyed both the

giant, and the dry bottom of the pool at the edge of Great Valley Lake.

'It's perfect,' he said. 'The glass in spectacles helps people to see because it is made slightly curved. The picture of the outside world is bent by the glass before the eye even sees it. The bottom of the lake is exactly the right curve. When the glass is melted by the fire and then cools and sets hard, it will be exactly the right curve for the giant's eyesight.'

All of the members of the court and the royal guard and the people of the Plain Green Plains piled half the windowpanes into the lake, and half the wood on top. Then they lit the wood and let it burn and burn for two whole days and nights. All the children

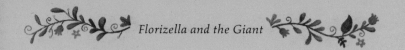

from Great Valley Lake School took another couple of days off without asking and had a barbecue round the lakeside that went on for two and a half days.

They had never had a summer like it.

After two days and two nights, the fire burned down and the glass, which had melted under the heat, started to set again in the shape of the pool – flat on top and perfectly curved on the bottom. When the royal surveyor brushed the grey wood ash away, the glass had melted into a smooth surface like ice on a pond.

Very carefully, without breaking it, they levered the glass from the bed of the pool and laid it on the soft grass of the Plain

Green Plains. Then they put in the rest of the windowpanes and melted those too – and all the children from Great Valley Lake School took another couple of days off without permission.

When they had finished, they had two giant lenses for spectacles so big and so thick that it took ten

men to carry each one.

All that was left to do *then* was for the nearby blacksmiths to come with their fire and their forges, and heat and hammer the twiddly bits from

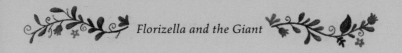

the fancy garden gates into a smart but simple pair of frames for the spectacles.

Six blacksmiths rolled up in their blackened and dirty wagons and put all their forges

together to make one really big hot fire. And all the blacksmiths' sons and daughters – who also should have been in school –

puffed on the bellows and made the charcoal glow a bright and brilliant red. Then the blacksmiths took all the old scrap metal and hammered and bashed it, cooled it down and heated it up, twisted it and forged it, knotted it together and smoothed it out until . . .

'That is really great,' said Princess Florizella with enormous relief.

It had been nearly a week since they'd first met the giant, and in all that time Florizella had been riding Jellybean up to the lake, and back to the royal camp, then off around the countryside to find more blacksmiths and more metal, as well as finding more food for the giant.

That was the bit that Samson liked the

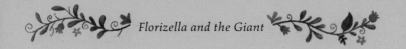

best. He always sat beside the giant at meal-times. He had never eaten so well in his life. Crumbs of bread and cake the size of boulders fell around him. Scraps of meat pies or cheese as big as cartwheels came tumbling down. Samson was the only one in the whole kingdom who was enjoying the giant's stay. He thought Giant Simon was just wonderful. In fact, he wished he would stay forever.

Three times a day Bennett sounded a horn and the whole area around the giant was cleared of every person and every animal for at least a kilometre, and Simon stood up and stretched and paced about for a little while. Only Cecilia stayed with him while he moved. He had a little pocket in his shirt where he tucked her inside, to keep her safe.

'Aren't you frightened of him?' Bennett asked her. She was, after all, such a very little girl.

'Thilly,' she said scornfully. 'You thilly printh! Thimon ith an abtholute thweety-pie.'

Bennett had to cough and go behind a tree again. But Florizella's mind was on the glasses, which were rumbling towards them on a specially built wagon drawn by ten big plough horses. Trailing a plume of chalky white dust behind it, the wagon came down the road towards the giant.

'I think I can see it!' the giant called. 'I think I can see the wagon coming! I see a white blob coming along the road!'

'Hold still! Hold still!' Florizella shrieked as the giant boots stamped the ground in

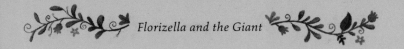

excitement. 'Stand still, Giant Simon!'

The giant obediently froze – but if you looked upwards you could see his thick green-socked knees trembling with excitement.

'I think I can see my glasses!' he said as quietly as he could manage. 'On a big cart. Are they really going to make me see everything clearly?'

'Yes!' Florizella said, with her fingers crossed behind her back for luck.

'And then you can go home and plant your own food,' Bennett reminded him.

'And no one will ever call you stupid again,' Florizella said encouragingly.

The wagon drew to a halt at the giant's feet. Simon bent down very carefully, putting Cecilia on the ground beside Florizella and Bennett. Then he picked up the spectacles by

the frames and looked at them.

'Put them carefully on your nose,' Florizella urged.

There was a long exciting silence while the giant settled them on his nose, pushed the arms of the spectacles into his curly fair hair and tucked them behind his huge ears.

He gazed out across the Plain Green Plains. 'I can see!' he said softly. 'I can see properly at last. It's lovely. I can see the hills and the mountains behind them. I can see the trees.'

He turned his big face to look downwards. 'And I can see my friends,' he began . . .

Then he screamed in absolute terror – so loudly that Florizella, Bennett, Cecilia and all the royal court were blown over and over by the blast.

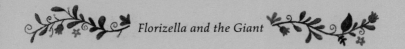

'Humans! Humans! *Ugh!* Humans! I hate humans! I thought you were mice!'

'Stand still! Stand still!' Florizella and Bennett yelled as the giant clumsily tried to jump away from the royal camp while the king and queen and the royal surveyor and the whole court clung to bushes and trees as the whole world shook around them. 'You'll hurt us! Stand still!'

The plough horses threw up their heads and bolted in ten different directions. Their driver leaped clear of the wagon, which overturned and was dragged zigzagging wildly away. People ran screaming with terror as the mighty boots crashed down first in one spot and then another like great unpredictable thunderbolts. High, high above them, above

the tops of the trees, they could hear the roaring complaints of the frightened giant.

'I hate humans! I hate humans! They're 'orrible! 'Orrible! I hate them. They're dangerous! They're nasty! They're sneaky! They come after you when you ain't done nothing! 'Orrible! 'Orrible!'

'*Stand still!*' Florizella yelled. 'Stand still and listen for a moment!'

The giant forced himself to stand still, quivering all over with fright.

'We're not 'orrible,' Florizella said. 'I mean horrible. We've been kind to you – remember? We've made you these spectacles and it took all the glass from our windows and all the iron in the kingdom! We've fed you every day! We're not sneaky and nasty!'

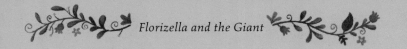

The giant shook his head. He was hopelessly confused.

'Cecilia is a human,' Florizella gabbled at the top of her voice. 'And you like her. She tells you wonderful stories. And you like Bennett – he brought you lemonade when you were thirsty. And you like me – and all of us here. We've fed you for a week. We've cared for you.'

The giant shook his head. 'I don't believe you! I've heard all about your sort! It was one of your tricks – being nice to me. I know all about humans! You'd have tied me up when I was asleep or something sneaky like that! You'd have come climbing up beanstalks after me! You'd steal my gold or set other giants on me! Well, you watch out, Princess Florizella!

Fee-fi-fo-fum, you know! I am a giant after all! I can grind your bones, don't forget!

Fee-fi-fo-fum!

Fee-fi-fo-fum!

I can't remember how the rest of it goes . . . *Umpty, umpty, umpty um!*'

He finished the last *Umpty, umpty, umpty um!* with a great roar, trying very hard to hide his own fear and to frighten everyone else.

'What are we going to do?' Florizella asked Bennett in an urgent whisper. 'If he goes on about grinding bones, the royal guard won't like it at all! And then we'll have a little war on our hands.'

'A giant war, you mean,' Bennett said. 'And *we've* given him spectacles so he can see us.

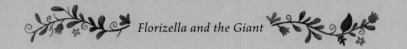

We won't have a chance if he attacks!'

Florizella looked behind her. Already people were getting up and looking for weapons, and mustering around the king and queen. They all looked angry and frightened. The royal guard gathered at the royal standard with their hands on their swords. The captain of the royal guard was setting out a battle plan. The drummer girls were looking for their drumsticks in a hurry in case anyone wanted to sound the retreat – or even advance. The queen beckoned urgently to Florizella to come to her. Florizella smiled pleasantly and waved back, pretending not to understand.

Suddenly, little Cecilia pushed between Florizella and Bennett.

'Lift me up!' she demanded. 'Lift me up on your thoulder.'

Bennett picked her up. She was still only as high as the giant's laces on his monstrous boots.

'*Thimon!*' she yelled. 'Giant Thimon! Can you hear me?'

The giant stopped still at her commanding little squeak.

'Yes,' he said a little more softly. 'I can hear you, Thethilia.'

'You are a big thilly to thpeak to Florithella like that,' she said severely. 'She hath been ath nithe ath she could be. And then you thtart up with thith *fee-fi-fo-fum* nonthenth. You thould be athamed of yourthelf. You are a great big naughty thing.'

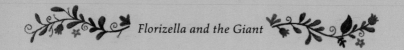

'I . . .' the giant began, but it was no use. Cecilia was quite unstoppable.

'Now, you thay thorry,' she said firmly. 'Or no one ith going to talk to you.'

There was a long silence.

'THAY THORRY!' Cecilia shouted with infinite threat.

'Thorry,' the giant said. 'Thorry. I was startled. I've never talked to humans before. I thought you were all horrid little vermin. A race of burglars and killers. Beansprout climbers. I thought you were all called Jack.'

'That's just a fairy story,' Florizella said. 'You don't want to believe everything you read in fairy stories.'

'Sorry,' the giant said more softly. 'I thought it was true. I thought we were natural enemies.'

Bennett shook his head. 'There are no natural enemies,' he said. 'You can always be friends if you choose to be. We'd like to be friends with you.'

The giant shuffled his feet rather dangerously.

'I'm sorry,' he said again very humbly. 'I want to be friends. I was very frightened for a moment, that was all.'

'That'th better,' Cecilia said firmly.

The giant bent down and put out his big warm hand. The three children climbed into it. He lifted them up and up and up, past the tree trunks, past the high branches of the trees, past the birds' nests and the tops of the trees, up to his face.

His big blue eyes were huge

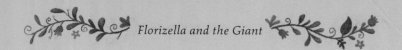

behind his new glasses, as big as two blue harvest moons. The effect was quite startling: Florizella found she was gazing and gazing into his deep, enormous eyes.

'I *am* sorry,' he said again. 'I know you're nice now. But I was always taught that humans were dreadful.'

'There are good and bad,' Cecilia ruled. 'Jutht like giantth, jutht like all people. Good and bad.'

Florizella and Bennett exchanged an amazed look.

'This Cecilia is one smart little girl,' Bennett whispered to Florizella. Aloud he said, 'If you are ready to leave, Giant Simon, then we have seeds and plants for you.' He pointed towards the horizon where there was a long train of carts loaded with sacks of tomato seeds, lettuce seeds, carrot seeds, potato seeds, marrow seeds, cucumber seeds, corn on the cob seeds and parsnip seeds. Behind them were more

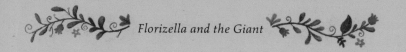

wagons piled high with little fruit trees, their branches tossing with the rolling of the carts along the road.

The giant gave a little sigh of pleasure. The three children grabbed on to his thumb and no one was blown away.

'That's a wonderful sight,' he said. 'It's very kind of you all. I shall take them home and plant them, and my garden will be the best of all gardens. And then I shall have friends who will come round to see it. They won't call me stupid then! They'll be pleased to know me!'

He bent down and put the children softly on the ground. With delicate fingers, he picked the tiny vegetables out of the carts and looked at them carefully. He could see them properly at last.

'These are grand!' he said. 'Grand. I'm very, very grateful to you all.'

'It's our pleasure,' the king said graciously. 'And now I think it is probably time for you to go, Giant Simon.'

It was a little unfortunate that everyone nodded very enthusiastically at the prospect of the giant leaving.

'We will be sorry to lose you,' the queen said tactfully, 'but I expect you will want to be getting back to your garden. Autumn is coming. You will want to be getting the ground ready for your crops.'

'We'll point you in the direction of your home,' Bennett said. 'You came from the west, from over the mountains.'

The giant had gone very quiet.

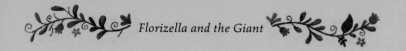

'We'll send the wagons along behind you,' Florizella said cheerfully. 'They can follow you until they reach our borders, and then you can carry the seeds and trees the rest of the way.'

The giant said nothing. He sighed deeply. All the flags at the royal camp streamed out in the wind of his sigh. A few tents blew over.

'Watch out,' Bennett said to Florizella. 'I think he's off again!'

A fat solitary tear crashed down into the bushes beside the two children, like a single massive wave on a beach.

'Don't cry!' Florizella yelled desperately. 'What's the matter?'

'Hold the horses!' Bennett shouted to the royal camp.

'Fasten down the tents!' The captain of

the guard turned to her force. 'Prepare for a storm!'

'*Unh-hunh!*'

The ground rocked with the giant's sob.

'*Unh-hunh! Unh-hunh!*'

'What *is* it?' Florizella shouted upwards.

'I'm going to miss you!'

The giant was bawling like a baby.

'I'm going to have to go back to my own country all by myself, and no one will tell me stories there.'

Tears cascaded down upon the children and the royal camp like a hurricane, like a typhoon. The giant's sobs uprooted great trees, a tent was washed away, several flagpoles were snapped off and the banners flew off in the gale of his cries.

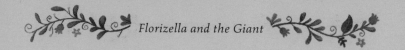

'Take cover!' the captain commanded and the guard took up the brace position for hurricanes.

High above the noise, a little voice was raised. '*Thtop it!*' said Cecilia indignantly. 'A great big giant like you! You should be athamed of yourthelf!'

Abruptly the giant stopped crying.

'You are too big to be thquealing and thnivelling all the time,' Cecilia said firmly. 'Bethideth, there ith no need for it. I am coming back with you to your country. I have athked my mum and she thayth I can. We can plant your garden together. I will thtay with you till the end of the thummer holidayth. And Florithella and Bennett will vithit you when you are thettled again.'

'Will you?' the giant asked. 'Will you come

with me, Thethilia? Stay with me until the end of the summer? And will you visit me, Florizella and Bennett?'

The children shouted, 'Yes, of course! Of course we will!' and watched anxiously as the giant carefully lifted his new glasses and wiped the last tears from his eyes with the back of his hand.

'I tell you what! We'll have a party to see you off!' the king shouted up. 'I expect you'd like some fireworks, wouldn't you? A nice jolly farewell party?'

'With hats?' Giant Simon asked eagerly. 'And things that you blow that squeal? And streamers? And games?'

Florizella and Bennett looked at the king.

'Oh, Daddy, look what you've done,'

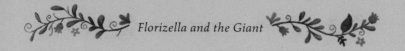

Florizella said reproachfully. 'How on *earth* are we going to make him a party hat? Or a blower?'

'Sorry,' the king said. 'I was just thinking of the royal enchanter's spectacular show.'

'Oh yes!' Florizella said delightedly. 'It's not like any party you've ever seen before!' she yelled up at the giant. 'No hats, but the most wonderful things! You just wait till you see it!'

The royal enchanter stepped forward. His magic blue coat billowed around him, and his tall pointy hat was slightly askew. 'An amusing little something?' he asked the king with a smile.

'Something for the children,' the king said. 'They've been so good!'

The royal enchanter produced a long silvery

wand from his drooping sleeve and tapped it lightly on the ground. At once a white marble fountain sprang out of the ground, bubbling and flowing with raspberry soda. Fireworks leaped out of the grass and whizzed up into the evening sky, popping and twinkling in a million different colours. The showboat, which had caught the king's fancy earlier, came pounding up the road with its paddles turning and very loud music, and dancing on the top deck.

A dozen incredibly fast, incredibly slippery water-slides appeared from nowhere and the children from Great Valley Lake School (*never* had they had such a summer!) dashed for them

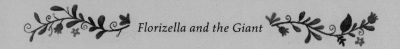

and flung themselves, still fully dressed, up the steps and then screaming, round and round, head over heels, down the water-slides. A little steam engine with carriages came chuffing up the road and high-kicking dancers wrapped in feather boas sprang out of every door and danced up and down. A thousand parachutes opened in the sky above them and a regimental brass band floated down playing ragtime jazz, never missing

a note, even when they dropped to the ground and rolled.

High on the crest of a billowing blue wave, a dozen world-class surfers came dipping and wheeling, riding the high plumes of sea spray through the little forest.

'Now *that's* what I call a spectacle!' the royal enchanter said to the royal surveyor with a superior sort of smile.

But Florizella had something on her mind. She looked around the crowd of delighted faces until she saw Cecilia's mother. She was laughing and pointing at a circus that had just arrived. There were unicorns doing a water ballet in rainbow-coloured water, with flying horses dipping

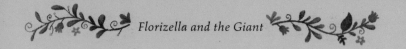

and wheeling around rose-pink fountains.

'I say,' Florizella asked her. 'Is it really all right for Cecilia to go with the giant?'

'Oh yes,' the girl's mother said with a smile. 'She's always been a great one for pets, has Cecilia. She'll stay till he's settled in and then she'll come home again. I let her go away for the holidays as long as she is back in time for school.'

'Pets?' Florizella asked. 'Does Cecilia call Giant Simon a pet?'

'Oh yes,' the woman said. 'Now all my children want one.'

Florizella shook her head. 'I just hope it doesn't become a craze.'

'Let them go, Florizella,' Bennett said. 'If she has decided that Giant Simon is her pet,

then she'll insist on keeping him. I'd rather she went with him than kept him here. That is one little girl who always gets her own way!' He cupped his hands round his mouth and shouted upwards. 'Well, goodbye, Giant Simon. We'll come and see you in the autumn.'

'Goodbye!' the giant boomed down at them. Fireworks exploded behind his head and he laughed delightedly. 'Goodbye, everyone, and thank you for everything, especially the party!'

'Tho long!' Cecilia called from high up in the giant's pocket. 'I'll be home in time for thchool in the autumn!'

The huge giant and the little girl in his pocket waved to the royal court and to Princess Florizella and Prince Bennett. Then, with the wagons of seeds and trees following behind

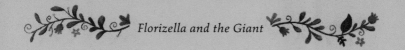

him, the giant turned westward into the pale apricot evening sunlight. Carefully he made his way home, treading on nobody, stumbling into nothing, watching where he put his huge feet and looking with pleasure all around him. As he walked, everyone could hear the piping voice of Cecilia going on and on and on with her unending stories.

They all watched him until he was a long way off, stepping carefully along the white track of the road as if it were a chalk line drawn for a game. The fireworks and the rockets, the parachuting band and the showboat and the train and the circus followed him into the distance and then faded from sight as a dream trickles away when you wake. When the giant was nothing more than a small moving dot on the horizon, everyone breathed a sigh of relief and started packing up the royal camp.

'I really liked that giant,' Florizella said. 'I'm glad we were able to make spectacles for him.'

'And give him seeds for his plants,' Bennett said. 'We could ride over to fetch Cecilia at the end of the summer holidays and see how his garden is getting on.'

'It's been a good adventure,' Florizella said.

'Yes,' Prince Bennett replied. 'Well done, Florithella.'

'Thuper,' she said with a grin.

The End